Renato After Alba

Renato After Alba

His Rage Against Life,
Love & Loss
in his own Words

Eugene Mirabelli

McPherson & Company

Published by McPherson & Company,
Post Office Box 1126, Kingston, NY 12402
www.mcphersonco.com

ISBN 978-1-62054-026-8

Library of Congress Cataloging-in-Publication Data

Names: Mirabelli, Eugene, author.
Title: Renato After Alba : his rage against life, love & loss in his
    own words / Eugene Mirabelli.
Description: Kingston, NY : McPherson & Company, 2016.
Identifiers: LCCN 2016032880 | ISBN 9781620540268 (alk. paper)
Subjects: LCSH: Older men—Fiction. | Painters—Fiction.
Classification: LCC PS3563.I68 R44 2016 | DCC 813/.54—dc23
LC record available at https://lccn.loc.gov/2016032880

Printed on pH neutral paper.

The author and publisher express thanks to the editor and staff of

New England Review, where a selection from *Renato After Alba* was

first published in the 2016 spring issue.

for Margaret

& the children

& the children's children

I WENT TO THE DAILY GRIND CAFÉ AND HAD A CUP of coffee at the little table where we often sat, but Alba didn't turn up, smiling and saying "I thought I'd find you here."

Because she is dead — I know, I know. What I don't know is where she went and why she hasn't come back and is she someplace I can get to without dying, because though I wanted to die and told myself over and over to die, it became clear it wasn't going to happen right away. I don't understand why we're born or why we love or why we bring children into the world if we and everyone we love are going to die.

❦

I was born at my grandfather's house in Lexington, Massachusetts, in the evening of the last snowfall of March, eighty-three years ago. You could say I was born a few days earlier, but on that snowy evening I was found in a laundry basket on my grandfather's doorstep, so that's my true birthday. My grandfather's big square house was on one side of St. Brigid's Church, and the small narrow parish house was on the other side. Everyone said I had been brought to the wrong door, but maybe my guardian angel directed the delivery to this address so that a newly married couple at the table that evening could adopt me and be my true parents, as did happen.

My grandfather's name was Pacifico Cavallù and there were fifteen people in the house that night. He was at the head of the table, a sturdy man with a short, iron-colored beard, and his wife Marianna sat opposite him, a glorious woman such as you find carved on the prow of an old sailing ship. Their children, handsome and headstrong, were seated on both sides of the long table — Lucia and Marissa and Bianca and Candida and Dante and Sandro and Silvio and Mercurio and Regina, along with Marissa's husband Nicolo, an aeronautical engineer, and Bianca's husband Fidèle, a stonecutter. And, of course, there was Carmela the cook and Nora the housemaid. That's two in the kitchen, thirteen at the table, and me in a laundry basket being set down quietly on the piazza.

Then came that KNOCK, KNOCK, KNOCK, so Pacifico got up from the table, his linen napkin still tucked into the top of his vest, and strolled through the grand front hall and into the vestibule to open the front door. *Good God!* he cries. At the table they drop their silverware and knock over chairs to come running and I am born.

❧

Four years later, here's my grandfather, my nonno, kneeling down to crush me against his scratchy vest and gold watch chain, kissing the top of my head, the air scented with bay rum cologne and Parodi cigars and filled with his *ho-ho-ho* when he lifted me up, up, too far up to the ceiling, then caught and lowered me and set me on my feet, and I ran to my mother. Nonno kept big barrels of wine sleeping on their stomachs in the dark cobweb cellar, which was two steps down from the big cellar, and the floor in the little cellar was dirt like outside.

Later, when I was six or seven, Floria led me and our cousin Nick over the low stone wall into the old burying ground and Floria said, "Look, you can lift up the slates," and she lifted a gravestone straight up so you could see the bottom edge, damp and sharp like a spade covered with dirt. "See?" she said. "We can switch them around." She switched two gravestones, then switched them back. In those days nobody died except the people from long ago who were already dead, like the people in that old graveyard, like Isaac Stone from 1690. Then we heard aunt Lucia, Floria's mother, calling, "Floria, vieni, vieni qui, Floria, andiamo! Andiamo!" So we climbed over the little stone wall and into Nonno's backyard where my father and uncle Nicolo and uncle Zitti were playing bocce in the big afternoon sunshine seventy-seven years ago.

❧

Now people die every day. Alba died on the first day of spring. She had caught a slight cold, we thought, but in the third night her cries woke me and I called 911 and the emergency team came. They took her blood pressure. "How often do you have atrial fibrillation?" someone asked her. She could barely sit in the chair without falling off. They put her on the gurney, maneuvered her down the stairway and into the EMS truck and we drove to the hospital emergency entrance. Then hours of agony and panic — her heart racing, blood pressure collapsing, kidneys failing, her gut in agonizing knots, blood turning to acid in her veins — they gave me a tiny sponge on a stick to wet her lips and mouth. "I can't stand pain the way you can," she gasped to me, then her tongue failed to obey her will she couldn't speak her eyes filled with terror, so that

and torture for twenty hours and her heart stopped. They pounded and heaved on her chest, trying to restart it, then backed off and used voltage, again and again and again and again and again, until the doctor said it was over and I rushed to grab her — "Oh, my beautiful Alba!" — got my arms around her to help her, to help her lift, help her get up from that bed, my cheek pressed to her warm breast, her sweet warm breast. Perspiration had suffused her face but, oh, she was so heavy as never in this life. Our children gathered drifted gathered here there, our children, our kids. I stroked her hair the way she always liked and I peeled away the bloody tapes and began to pull the tube from her mouth, when some busybody bitch rushed at me, saying, "No, no, not until the coroner comes!" The doctor was sitting on a small metal chair outside the glass room, writing on a long pad he held on his knees. He looked tired. He said Alba had succumbed to a bacterial infection. "You don't have to go," he told me. "You can stay with her as long, as long as you want." But it was no use, so I told him, "No. Her spirit is gone." Our kids took me home.

❦

That was my cousin Floria, leading us on adventures over the little stone wall to the old burying ground or up to the attic and beneath the slanting roof where the steamer trunks were stored, decorated with stickers from the White Star Line and the Cunard. A year or two later she gave me her writing desk, because she was going to the villa in Sicily with her mother Lucia and Nonno. The desk had ink stains on it, but when I lifted the lid it was clean inside and smelled fresh and I could keep drawing paper and pencils there. Everyone was calling to aunt Lucia, saying, "Hurry, hurry up, Lucia. We'll miss the boat! Andiamo!" But Lucia had stopped to light her cigarette. "The boat will wait!" she said, coming into the car, an airy scarf of smoke trailing over her shoulder. Dante and Regina were in the car ahead of us, and Nonno was the car ahead of them, and we all drove to Boston and walked up the gangway onto the ship to say goodbye. It was a bright sunny day. I don't recall if our cousin Veronica was with us, but Nick and I had a great time.

🐝

Now Nonno and aunt Lucia and Floria were at the villa in Palermo, but the rest of us still gathered every Sunday at the big house in Lexington, the same as ever, because Nanna was still there. After the long midday dinner, my father and uncle Nicolo and uncle Zitti would remain at the table with their wine and coffee and the adult aroma of tobacco smoke. Zitti and Nicolo were professors and whenever they disagreed about something they would turn to Fidèle, my father, and ask him to referee. The young uncles had no wives yet and were up on the third floor, trying to put together a bamboo fishing pole, or they were cleaning the guns — something like that. But then we heard them clattering down the stairs. Uncle Zitti and Uncle Nicolo were talking about politics or religion when Silvio and Mercurio came through the dining room, their riding boots booming on the floor. "We're going out to watch Sandro's hawk," Silvio said. "Anybody coming with us?"

"No," Mercurio told him. "They're going to sit there all day and discuss Roosevelt and Norman Thomas. Or Mussolini. Let's go."

"Tell Sandro to be careful," uncle Nicolo called after them. "That hawk is still wild."

"One of the neighbors is going to take a shot at that bird," my father murmured.

I had watched Sandro's hawk before and there wasn't much to watch; it had yellow eyes and it just flew up and around in circles, and then after a while it swooped down and landed on Sandro's arm, on his big leather glove, where he fed it. My cousin Nick said Come on, let's go outside, and I said Veronica wants to come, too. Nick went out and I would have gone with him, but now Uncle Nicolo asked Uncle Zitti what had God been doing before he created the universe — a funny kind of question and I wanted to hear the answer.

"Ah," Zitti said. He smiled and pressed the end of his silver cigarette case so it sprang open like a little book. "Saint Augustine has the answer to that one."

"And what does your Saint Augustine say?" Nicolo asked.

My father had rolled up his sleeve and tucked two walnuts into the crook of his arm, but now he paused, waiting for the answer.

"He says God was preparing hell for those who pry too deep."

My father gave a brief laugh and closed his arm, cracking the walnuts.

"Let me correct myself," Zitti said, tapping the end of his cigarette against the silver case. "Saint Augustine didn't say that, but he talks about somebody else who said that. Augustine himself takes the question seriously."

"Does he say who God is?" Nicolo asked. He had unfolded a dazzling white handkerchief and was polishing his glasses, a pair of small octogons, like Ben Franklin's bifocals.

Zitti turned to me. "Tell your Uncle Nicolo who God is," he said.

"God is the creator of heaven and earth and all things," I recited.

My father didn't say anything, but resettled himself comfortably in his chair, satisfied with my answer. He didn't go to church, nor did any of my uncles, but it was understood that I would learn the catechism and go to church every Sunday with my mother and my little brother Bart for a while longer.

"Did the universe create itself out of nothing?" Zitti asked Nicolo.

Nicolo had started to reply, but then caught himself and nodded in my direction — bringing me into the discussion, I thought. He put his glasses back on. "I don't know," he told Zitti.

"Exactly. Nothing can create itself out of nothing!" Zitti said, slapping the table in delight. "Thus, we have God. Q.E.D."

"Renato's a big boy," my father told uncle Nicolo. "You can talk in front of him."

"I'm not a philosopher," Nicolo said, sweeping his

hand here and there on the tablecloth as if to iron out the wrinkles, or maybe brush something away. "I'm an engineer, a believer in the scientific method. Science finds out the way the world is made and how it works. The more science explains, the less mysterious the world is, and the less mysterious it is, the less we use God to explain how or why things happen. I don't see evidence of God anywhere." He glanced at me and added, "But that's just my opinion."

"I see God everywhere I look," Zitti countered, flinging his arms out. "This world, the stars, the gravity that holds everything together — it didn't create itself. God created it."

"And who created God?" Nicolo asked him.

"Michelangelo created God!" my father announced. He drained his wineglass and banged it down on the table. "Sistine Chapel. Fantastic work. Genius!"

I ran out and climbed over the little stone wall into the old graveyard, but by then Nick and Veronica were already going out the other side, down into the big meadow. In the field the air was extra warm and sweet with the scent of freshly mown hay, and when you looked up it was all sky and Sandro's hawk making circles higher and higher toward the sun.

❧

I couldn't endure the thought of Alba shut in a narrow coffin, and that coffin in a concrete box lowered into a hole in the ground and then dirt shoveled on it.

I let her body go clothed in one of her favorite dresses, one I loved, sky-blue with a narrow waist, let her body go up in⁣　　　and received her ashes in a heavy stone box, carried her in my arms against my chest to the car, and I held her while Skye drove us home in the silence, because neither of us could speak. When we had closed the front door, my daughter said, "I think we need a hug," and we hugged. Her ashes are like her dress; they are not her.

🐝

Time after time I cried Die. But it didn't work and I didn't die.

🐝

Scott came over to take me for a walk, because I hadn't been out of the house. He must have phoned first and Skye must have said Yes, come over, or maybe I told him Yes, because here he was and we went out. I turned up the collar of my barn jacket, buttoned everything and jammed my hands in the pockets, because I knew how to do that. My legs walked and I got a little way down the road and already I was tired and when I looked around I discovered that everything was actually fake — the flat housefronts standing beside the road had nothing behind them, the empty trees, the papery cutout clouds against the fake blue sky — all rigged up like a cheap stage set. I stopped and told him, "Everything's fake. Look at it! It's bogus, all of it." Scott said, "Where? What do you mean?" I said, "All this. See?" And I pointed to the houses and the black trees. "It's all made to look real, but it's all pretend and make-believe." He looked at me, then he said, "Let's keep walking. Where do you want to walk to?" I said I didn't know, so he said, "Let's go this way," and we turned down some other road. The road was level but it felt like it was uphill and I was getting more and more tired. We kept walking and walking. I told him, "It's not right. It's not right. Her dying, it's not right." Scott didn't say anything and we kept walking. It was a hard walk. I said, "If there's no God, who tortured her to death?" Finally he said we could go back to the house, so we turned around and headed to the house. I said, "It's not right, her dying. It's not right, Scott," and Scott didn't say anything until he said, "I know. It's not right."

Another day it was Fletcher who came to take me for a walk. It must have been windy because he said,

"Let's go this way and when we come back to the house the wind will be behind us." You could see how the trees and houses were fake and I was about to say it was weird how people could live in them, because they were no thicker than cardboard cutouts, but I decided not to because he'd think I was crazy. We walked along and I told him it wasn't right, Alba's dying. Fletch gave up a long sigh and cleared his throat and said, "Yes, it was terrible." "It wasn't right," I said. "God tortured her for twenty hours until she died," I told him. Fletch hung his head and walked along looking mostly at his boots and after a while he said, "I could help you fix that chair in the living room, the one with the loose leg." I said that was good. Yes, I wanted to do that. "I'll bring my clamps the next time I come," he said, straightening up. We agreed on that.

Zoe came over to take me for a walk and when we were walking I showed her the houses and the trees and the sky, showing her how it was all made-up fake. "See. It's not real. It's a scam." Zoe looked older than usual and said, "Yes." I knew that if you go to the side of a house the front disappears from view, and then it's the side that's only as thick as a sheet of cardboard, so everything is still fake, but I knew better than to talk about it. We walked along and everything was crazy because Zoe is the mother of my third child, Astrid, but it was Alba who brought her up, and here I was walking with Zoe, and Alba was gone and everything was wrong, like Zoe wearing high-heel shoes while we were walking on this rural road with its crumbling tar, pebbles and sand. A gusty wind blew through with a spatter of raindrops, making Zoe hunch her shoulders; she looked to be freezing but she kept walking beside me. Long ago, Zoe and Alba and I were young and foolish and fooling around, the three of us together one summer, and that's how Astrid got born, but nothing makes any sense now.

Zoe and Scott and Fletcher came over every so often, each alone, to take me for a walk. I marveled how they knew to take me for a walk.

I don't know what I did the first month. My daughters Skye and Astrid came, and my son Brizio, too, of course; sometimes they were all here together, sometimes only my son or one of my daughters, then they were gone and only my oldest daughter, Skye, was here. She was here for two weeks, of which I can recall nothing; then she left and Astrid came and I don't remember anything of those two weeks, either. I'm amazed they didn't go crazy, dwelling with their living-dead father. I do recall the memorial service. And I remember after the service, when all who had come were together around me, and grief had loosened their hearts and they shared this love, all of them, and as long as they talked and ate and drank and talked, just that long would Alba be here among us, but they had lives to get back to, and one by one they went and the spaces grew larger and finally they had all gone and there was only empty space. That evening Brizio returned to his home and I was by myself.

❦

One day I carefully opened the drawers in the night-stand and scooped out the shimmering black satins, airy silks, straps and hooks and collars, crammed everything into a small white trash bag, leaving a breath of warm perfume in the air, and then I took down the shoe-box from the closet shelf and poured a quiet jingling tumble of soft leather, silvery buckles, chains and rings into the trash bag. I closed the bag with two ties and carried it down to the garage where the trash barrels stood waiting. Next, I brought a larger trash bag up-stairs and opened her closet and gathered all the shoes and put them carefully, two by two — and those pre-cious gold sandals with the imprint of her slender foot — put them into the bag and closed it with two ties and shut the closet door. I couldn't touch the dresses. I carried the bag down to the garage and lowered it care-fully into the barrel beside the other one. Then I went to her desk where she had idly set her purse, which no one had touched since. I gently emptied it onto the writ-ing surface and tenderly separated out her lipsticks, the door keys and the car key, an eyebrow pencil, a mir-ror, crumpled paper tissues, her miniature address book, two pens, a nail file, magnifying glass, a small Floren-tine leather purse with change inside, a small pad of notepaper, three postage stamps, a few safety pins, and all her little private things. Afterward, there was plenty of time to sit on the foot of the bed to howl and sob.

❧

I made a list of my friends and jotted down the date whenever I phoned them, so I wouldn't call anyone too often. Almost nobody phoned me. But Susan Salter called and suggested dinner at a restaurant, said she'd pick me up, drive us there and back. She was a friend of Alba's from Art New England (good-looking, witty, many lovers, never married and slightly crazy), she arrived wearing what she knew Alba would have worn — a white summer dress and a splash of color — but with more jingling jewelry on her arm than Alba wore in a lifetime. We weren't really friends and didn't have much to talk about, but I appreciated how she was trying to help me get through the day. Al Levine phoned and we went to lunch, though we knew each other only slightly and had never had lunch or even a coffee together. John Duffy phoned from Philadelphia. He and David had been living together almost as long as Alba and I, so he understood and we had a good talk. I went to lunch in Cambridge with George Agathos. We've enjoyed boisterous dinners with George and Io — quantum mechanics and Greek cooking — but now George was so concerned about me he looked ten years older. Zocco and his wife invited me to Sunday brunch with mutual friends, but it would have been too many people for me to deal with. I had dinner with Zoe and Emerson every so often, because after me and our children, no one missed Alba more than Zoe. When she learned about Alba, she came to the house, frightened and white-faced, and when she hugged me it was as if she were clinging for support. Now it was just me and Zoe and Emerson at their table, which was friendly and calm. Avalon and Sebastian had me over for dinner, too. Avalon, whose story with me is too complicated to tell right now, seated me at the head of the table and made pasta puttanesca the way I had taught her. Their kitchen is always full of Sebastian's bright cut-paper art and I like being distracted that way. Nils Petersen was good to be with but he had received a grant and was off with his wife Hanna doing avant-garde computer art, or whatever they call it, in the Netherlands. Every so often, Fletcher or Scott would phone and say let's have lunch, so I saw them from time to time.

I drove to the Daily Grind café once or twice a week, the way we used to, and when I'd get out of the car it felt as if Alba was here, walking beside me the same as ever. At the café I trade a few words with Garland behind the counter, or whoever is around, then I go talk with Gordon. At the memorial service it had been painful to see him not in his white apron with its smudges of coffee dust, but in a stiff black suit and black necktie, because something terrible had happened to Alba. He still talks about politics or sports or hard times in the coffee business, and how he misses his old location in Boston. Sometimes I talk about Alba, and he listens and doesn't try to change the subject. Or I sit alone at the window, when that's what I feel like doing. Once I was sitting by the window watching it rain and I felt Alba come up behind me, as she sometimes did at home, to kiss my cheek, so I leaned back and turned my cheek toward her, not that I thought she was there, but because I wanted her to know that I felt her presence and loved her. Walking back to the car I always think about Alba and I want to have died.

☙

Sometimes it was me who had died and Alba who was living and I'd see her walking solitary in the quiet before sunset, walking slowly along the empty sidewalk in the little college town where Skye and her family have their home, or I'd see her at the table in our kitchen where she had set out two or three yellow place mats, but only one dish, eating alone in the silent kitchen, and my heart would contract in pain.

☙

While Alba's possessions — her dresses, her little bottles of perfume and cologne, small jars of lotion, her glasses — were charged with meaning, all the other things in the house made no sense. The pewter bowls we had arranged on the fireplace mantel, the Afghan carpets we'd bought from Morgan, every worn book in the bookcase and the Italian tiles we had set into the kitchen wall, those things had no more meaning

or connection to me than items on display in a house-
ware shop.

🌱

There wasn't anything to do, so I went out to the
studio. The ancient barn collapsed the day we had
our first picnic out here, so we'd built a new one with
big windows up high all around and a studio loft at
the back that faced over the fields toward the woods.
Years ago I had begun some frescos — the real thing
on a mix of ground-up limestone and volcanic sand.
I planned to build them into the walls and the barn
would become a chapel of earthly delights — or so I
had thought, if you can call it thinking. A few frescos
leaned against the walls, rotting like everything else.
Eventually I gave up on them and returned to canvas,
lots of canvas. Now the studio floor creaked underfoot because I hadn't been up there for weeks. A big
flat crate still stood by the door. I had packed three
paintings for a group show in Worcester, but after
Alba   I didn't send it. I phoned the gallery,
dropped out of the show and didn't send the crate.
The sketches tacked to the walls had died, and the
stretchers leaning here and there, the table, the jars
and brushes — everything was dead. Photographs
of Alba stayed on the shelf by the table, but they
weren't true anymore. I opened a window and sat
for a while, but there was nothing to do, so I closed
the window and left.

❦

I had kept hoping to die but it hadn't happened and after a while I gave up trying and pretended to live, just doing the things that living people do. I got up and shaved and showered and got dressed in fresh clothes. I shopped for food every day, mostly just to leave the empty house. Nadeau's grocery was nearer, but Big Valley Farms was larger and extra-bright inside and there were lots of people to be around. When I got out of the car in the big parking lot I'd haul myself up straight to show I was Alba's husband and proud of it. It was hard to do. I kept my back straight and my face up, because she had loved me of all this whole world. Still, I would rather have been dead.

❦

I didn't know what to do with being alive. I remembered the young woman at the Barista Coffee stand whose husband had died and I thought she could tell me what to do. She was preparing coffee for me and Alba when I noticed the snake coiling down her bare white arm to her wrist, nicely tattooed in ashen blue color. The snake had Japanese kanji on it. I told her I admired the artwork, a polite lie, and asked what the Japanese writing said. "Cancer shits," she said, pressing the plastic lids onto our coffees. "It says cancer shits."

"Oh," Alba said. "I'm so sorry!"

The young woman had already turned aside and was

briskly polishing the coffee machine. "Not me. My husband," she added. By then somebody was standing behind us, waiting to order, so we left. The Barista stand was halfway to Cambridge and I bought coffee there maybe two or three more times after that. She had a thin whip-like body and black hair that stood up in thick soft spikes. She was good-looking, but like she had been punched in the face a few times and was making a slow recovery. I'd say, "How are things?" She'd give me half a laugh and answer, "Different day, same old shit." One time I asked her how her husband had died. "Brain cancer," she said.

"Oh, God, that's awful. I'm so sorry."

"Shit happens," she said.

"How long ago?"

"Eleven months," she said.

So now I went to the Barista stand and bought a cup of coffee, and when she handed it to me I spoke up like a crow trying to talk, saying, "My wife died and I don't know what to do." She looked straight at me a moment, then she said, "You can phone me. Will you call if I give you my number?" I croaked Yes. She scribbled her number on a slip of paper, slid it across the counter, saying, "Call me," then she looked to the customer behind me, so I headed to my car.

I didn't call her and I decided not to see her again, but stayed home at the window and watched the rain falling. But when it stopped raining I got in the car and drove out to the coffee stand, and as I was walking toward it I saw her coming down the wet sidewalk. She saw me and said, "You lose my number?" I said No, said I didn't want to bother her. "I don't let people bother me. — How are you doing?" she asked. I shrugged and said, "I don't know how I'm doing." People were bumping into me and brushing past us and a pelting rain had begun to fall.

"How did she die?"

We stepped into a doorway to get out of the rain and away from the people going by. I told her how Alba died and while I talked and cried, she stared out at the cars flashing by in the rain. I told her I was going crazy.

"Don't worry about it," she says, carefully drying her eyes with her fingers. "Crazy's all right. Crazy is a way to cope." She wore eyeliner, a thin black line along her eyelashes, but now it was muddy. I asked her what her name was. "Shannon," she says.

"Shannon what?"

"O'Hare."

She didn't ask but I told her my name anyway.

"Are you coming to buy a coffee tomorrow?" she asked.

I said Yes.

She looked at me a moment. "Is that a crappy yes or a real yes? Because you didn't call and you said you would, you know." I told her it was real yes and she said, "I gotta catch a bus," and went off. She was thin, like a knife.

The next day at the coffee stand she slid a red iron pan full of something heavy onto the counter and into a rumpled brown paper bag and said, "Take it."

"What is it?" I lifted the edge of the bag and caught the scent of tomato sauce.

"It's lasagna."

"Lasagna?"

"You got an Italian name, right? And you don't know lasagna?"

"You made me lasagna! You can't do that!"

"It's homemade, my kitchen."

"Christ."

"You have to eat more. That'll last you a few days."

A woman with two kids in tow had come up behind me, so I said thanks to Shannon and went home.

The lasagna's fiery tomato sauce had more pepper than I use in a month, and it lasted a week because I could swallow only a few forkfuls a day and by the last day the pasta strips had turned to leather. When I brought the iron pan back to her at the Barista Coffee stand, I told her it was great lasagna. "Good," she said. "Because you need to gain weight. You look hollow. You look like you got nothing inside."

❦

I received an announcement of Frank Vanderzee's exhibit at a gallery in Cambridge, and three days later a handwritten note arrived from Winona saying how especially happy they would be if I could come to the

opening, although, she added, they knew I was not going out much, which they did understand, but they
still hoped I could come. Vanderzee was maybe half as
old as I was. I liked his work and we had gone to each
other's shows for the last decade, but now the prospect
of entering a room crowded with chattering people
frightened and depressed me. I wasn't up to going by
myself so I asked Scott would he drive me there and,
if I needed to quit and leave without looking at anything, would he drive me right home. He said, "Sure.
When do you want me to pick you up?"

So I got to the gallery and looked around and when
Vanderzee saw me he came over. I told him I remembered when he was working on these canvasses and I
had liked them then, and I liked them even more now.
He smiled. "It's great to see you. I'm so glad you're
here." Winona came and put her arm gently through
mine and said, "There's a table with wine and cheese
at the other end of the room. Shall we go?" I said, Yes,
let's try that. I had a glass of wine and some crackers
and we chatted about the kids. I had to focus my mind
to make conversation, but I could do it. Gail came
up and gave me a cautious hug, as if I might shatter.
"Vanderzee and his wives," Alba used to say, though
he wasn't married to pale Winona or cinnamon Gail.

I liked Winona and Gail, but I felt strange standing there and every so often it felt like I was going to
tip over. Michiko, who had taught me all the kanji I've
since forgotten, and her husband Robert arrived and we

talked for a while. Michiko said she had been looking at photographs she took of Alba at our picnic last year and would make copies for me. Later I recognized Lucy Dolan, who used to babysit for us, just as she recognized me. She searched my eyes, and in a rush of sympathy threw her arms around me hard and held on like I don't know what. We talked for a moment or two — she said she was thinking of coming back to Boston now that her daughter was grown up and had left home. A few minutes later I saw Scott and asked him if he could drive me home now and he said, "Sure. Let's go." I said goodbye to Vanderzee and his wives and after I got home I sat at the kitchen table and howled, because of what God had done to Alba and how she suffered.

❦

The only widower I knew was Peter Panosian, a lawyer and amateur painter. He and his wife Helen were about fifteen years younger than we were. Helen was a vibrant woman, a prize-winning California surfer in her youth, and her slow dreadful dying had gnawed at Peter. He remained single for years, then around the time he retired he married the youngish legal assistant who had worked in his office for a decade. They moved to Pennsylvania, but we didn't lose touch and when he learned that Alba had died he wrote me a good note. So I phoned him. I think I said, Peter, this is Renato and I'm at a loss. My voice was so shaky I stopped talking, and Peter said, "Oh, Renato, oh, oh, oh." Then we talked for a while and he said, "Listen, I have to go to New York to give a talk on image and copyright — nowadays people think that whatever's on the Web is in the public domain. When I finish that business I'll come up to Boston. We'll have lunch." I said, No, that's too much trouble. He said, "No, it isn't."

So we had lunch in Boston. I think we talked for two hours, maybe more. Talking and listening to him gave me a certain relief, a sense of almost-sanity. After lunch we got into our coats and then lingered outside, talking a while longer, and he asked if I was painting. I said I hadn't picked up a brush since Alba died. "I painted a little every day," he said. "It was the only way I kept myself together. And it kept me close to her." I said I didn't see myself painting again ever. "I'm an amateur, you're an artist," he said flatly. We shook hands and embraced. "You'll paint," he told me as he headed off. I'd seen the paintings he did after his wife died. Peter liked bold primary colors, so his canvases were eye-catching, and each one was of his wife gazing straight out at you, like a series of self-portraits by Frida Kahlo. I suppose Frida had her reasons for painting that way, and I know Peter had his. The idea of painting made me sick.

☙

Everyone was kind to me, but if I talked about Alba and went on about her it made them uneasy. So I asked Shannon her schedule and drove to the Barista

Coffee stand every day to talk with her, because she didn't mind it when I talked a lot about Alba, and she didn't care if I was fifty years older than she was, and no matter what I said it didn't bother her. One day Shannon told me about Fitzpatrick, who had moved in with her a month ago. "He began hanging around," she said. "He delivers supplies for Barista. I told him, Listen, I'm not going to rearrange my place. I keep a photo of my husband in my living room and another in my bedroom, right by the bed. He says, I'm all right with that. Then he asks me, What do you want? So I told him and he says, I understand. — He thinks he does, but he doesn't," she added.

"What do you want?" I asked her.

"I want my old life back."

"Nobody understands that," I said.

"Nobody understands a fucking thing. Like at the funeral they all say, Just give me a call if you need anything. Then they disappear and I'm supposed to call up and plead with them for help. Why the hell don't they fucking phone me? What are they afraid of ?"

"They're afraid the person they love most might die." I stood at the end of the counter, looking down the street at the traffic. I asked what her husband's name was.

"Robert," she said. "Everyone called him Bob or Bobby, but I called him Robert, his real name. We did everything together. He was the best person I ever knew. — Here, I'll show you," she said, taking out her phone. She flicked through some photos, then handed me the phone — big smile on his face, reddish-gold hair, striped rugby shirt.

"He's handsome," I said. "And so young. What did you do at the beginning, after he died?"

Before Shannon could answer, a guy with a computer backpack stopped by, bought a coffee, went off.

"After three months I got this job," she said. "I was running out of money and you can't pay the rent with food stamps. At night I wrote him letters. I wrote every night. I have a stack this big. Have you tried writing her letters?" she asked me.

"Only notes. Just two or three sentences."

"Whatever works," she said.

🙥

A letter arrived from Leo Conti to remind me that some time ago I had said, yes, he could come out to look at my work with an eye to showing it in his gallery. Now he was wondering if I had finished those pieces which, he said, had sounded so wonderfully interesting to him, and when should he visit my studio. Leo is short and rather round, while his wife Elena is tall, large-boned, and rather handsome. They had come to the memorial service. That day he was in a black suit with a broad black necktie, but he wasn't wearing one of his assorted wigs and at first I didn't recognize him. He looked up at me searchingly for a long moment, sad bags under his eyes, then dropped his head and said nothing. His wife said, "We're so sorry, so very sorry, we loved her." I assured her that Alba had loved them, too.

If Leo died they'd need a giant corkscrew to dig his grave, the man is so crooked. He also has a true eye for talent and if he likes your work he finds people to buy it. Leo Conti had built a successful accounting firm (Conti, Cronin, Stein & Bradford) and then, maybe fifteen years ago, he sold his share to his partners and opened a large gallery in a former automobile repair shop in East Cambridge — cement floor, glass-brick windows and a mile of wall space. Alba told me Conti wanted to be known as a patron of the arts, not an accountant, and she said he liked my work and would probably take it. At the time, I was seventy and making an assault on the top Newbury Street galleries, trying to get back to where I had been when I had a name, so I avoided Conti and told Alba I wouldn't show in his morgue unless I was dead.

But, you know, I was dying by inches and had nothing to lose, so I invited him to my studio. He arrived in a white cotton jacket with broad rose stripes, a pink necktie, platform shoes and a head of fake curly black hair. He liked what he saw. In fact, he was crazy about my work. But the building that housed his gallery was being sold, he said, and he hadn't found a new place yet, was going broke and was doubtful about fitting me into his schedule. So I volunteered to pay for the advertising and reception and — *surprise!* — he fit me into his schedule. What I mean by crooked is that on the day my show opened I learned that Leo Conti owned the building and he was the one selling it, was making big money on the deal, and could have paid for everything a thousand times. But I must add that he found buyers and, subtracting what I had given him, I still made more from that single exhibit than I had in the previous five years combined.

After the exhibit, Leo told me he was planning to move his gallery to Boston and, in fact, to locate on Newbury Street — "Not exactly *on* Newbury, not geographically speaking, but 'off Newbury,' as they say, meaning around the corner, more or less." Six months later the Conti Gallery opened south of the South End, which is in Boston all right, but geographically farther from Newbury Street than when he was in East Cambridge. I exhibited with him there and again a few years later when he cut the distance to Newbury in half by moving his gallery to Back Bay, and I always made good sales. We had lunch maybe six months before Alba — before when, before — and I talked about some new works I had completed and that's when he told me he was angling for a place on Newbury Street. I asked him if he meant on Newbury Street *geographically*. He looked injured. "Yes, yes," he said, leaning back in his chair, his hand over his heart. "What do you take me for?" he asked. I didn't say.

Now I went out to my studio to look around again. The air in there was dead. Photographs of Alba waited on the shelf by my table. They refer to her but are not her. I looked at the big flat crate which held the three paintings that had been going to the Worcester show. I pried it open and hauled out the first stretcher and leaned it against the wall. I tried to view it, but the paint was meaningless and looking at it made me a little sick, so I slid it back into the crate and walked back to the house. I wrote a letter to Leo Conti, thanked him for asking about my work and told him I'd write again later. I couldn't paint and didn't want to.

❦

I could not believe in the loving God and be true to Alba, so God was swept away and I stayed with Alba. Alba loved me and loved our children. God could have taken instruction from her.

❦

We met when she was fourteen and I was seventeen. I was stacking crates of fish and ice on a dock in Newburyport when she came walking by with her arms full of long-stemmed flowers wrapped in green tissue paper. She asked me, Where's the *Saint Raphael*? and I pointed to where it was tied up and told her, That's it, the *Saint Raphael*, and she walked on. She came back later with the flowers gone and she looked at me, put her hand up to shade her eyes and looked at me, and I said, Renato Stillamare. She smiled — she had green-hazel eyes and the bridge of her nose was sunburned — then she looked away and kept walking. That evening I saw her out strolling with two other girls on the breakwater and when they saw me they nudged each other and giggled. The next night she was walking on the breakwater alone and I said, Hi, and she said, Hi, and I said, How old are you? and she said, Almost fifteen, and I laughed and said, Is that the same as fourteen? She looked off at the horizon and drew a strand of hair from her eyes, tucked it behind her ear and walked away. I caught up with her and said, Please, I really like you, I like you. So we walked along together and that's the way it began.

We went for walks and we talked. Her parents grew flowers and had a flower shop. I told her I was going to art school in September, because I was good at drawing and wanted to be an artist. She was good at languages and said she wanted to be a diplomat and travel abroad. We lay in the freshly mowed hayfield up back of her house, the stubble sharp and prickly. I had never made love before, but I let her think I knew what I was doing and we blundered through it. The next night she told me, I'm still bleeding. I didn't know what to do and we lay in the field with our arms around each other. After two days she stopped bleeding and we made love in the field every night, even if it was raining, and when we'd get up she'd rake her hand through her hair to comb out the bits of straw. She told me the secret Algonquin name she had named herself: Ka-gi-gi, the raven. I would think of her while

I was working and the first moment I'd see her in the evening I'd feel so strange, as if I had stepped off the dock and was falling, and I thought I was going crazy and was relieved when September came, because she went back to high school and I went off to the School of the Museum of Fine Arts in Boston.

❦

The other day I began by writing *Dear Alba* at the top, but it was impossible. As a matter of fact, I can't write you if I use stationery, which is why I've been using notepaper. All I want to say is they are re-doing Nadeau's Grocery. They've pushed out the back wall so it's bigger inside and they're putting in a new tile floor and bright lights everywhere. It looks a lot brighter. I know this is trivial and stupid, but I kept thinking Oh, I should tell Alba about this. Now I'm back from Nadeau's so I'm writing you this note. Don't worry, I know this is crazy.

❦

Scott phoned and asked did I want to have lunch someday this week. We ate at the Kitchen Table Restaurant, and when the waitress took our orders she told me, rather crisply, "Maybe you can finish your sandwich this time. You need to eat more." She was the thin one, middle-aged, named Lilian. I ordered only a half-sandwich, anyway. After she left, Scott asked me, "You come here often?"

"Not really," I said.

"She's right, you should eat more."

"I'm never hungry."

Scott hesitated, seemed about to speak, but didn't say anything. I told him, "You can't make up your mind whether to be sympathetic or critical."

"I think I'll change the subject," he said. "What do you want to talk about — sports, politics, philosophy, war, peace, the economy? How about the economy? What happened to money?"

"I haven't been keeping up with anything."

Scott sat back in his chair and studied me a moment. "How have you been?" he asked.

"I'm OK, I'm getting by. What about yourself?"

"Me?" He looked surprised. "I'm all right. My ankles were getting swollen, but my doctor reduced my blood-pressure medication and I'm fine now."

We talked about our blood-pressure medication until our waitress arrived with Scott's bratwurst and potato pancakes, and my half-sandwich which they'd purposely overstuffed. I remembered he had attended a conference in Boston a week ago, so I asked him about that. He made a brisk, dismissive gesture, as if brushing something away. "Papers and discussion groups on artificial intelligence, computers and thinking machines," he said. "Philosophers and mathematicians, mostly."

His career began in philosophy and took a turn into symbolic logic, and from there it branched into mathematics, thence computers and artificial intelligence. Now Scott, being Scott, quickly become bored by the conference discussion groups, so he went out to visit the neighborhood where he had grown up. That was Mattapan, which I should tell you is as far down the map as you can go and still be in Boston.

"I hadn't been down Blue Hill Avenue for fifty years," he told me. "And I knew I shouldn't go, but I was curious so I went. After the exodus, you know, the blacks moved in. African Americans, I mean. And Caribbeans." He paused and thought a moment. "It was a wonderful place to grow up in, years ago. And the street was lined with interesting stores and little shops. Sort of urban, but haimish. The past is memories," he decided.

It was on the tip of my tongue to tell him otherwise, but I said, "What did you do at the conference. You gave a talk, right? So how did it go?"

"Went well, I'm told." He shrugged. "Big discussion on free will. My point was that we don't have free will and if we ever get around to building a machine that thinks, it won't have free will, either."

"Are grown-up philosophers still arguing about free will? We did that in high school. No wonder you got bored. — By the way, I have free will unless someone puts a gun to my head."

"We disagree about that. — But the important thing is that I visited the scenes of my childhood. My past is intact. I have memories."

"Well-meaning people tell me I have memories of Alba. They think that's a comfort to me. They don't know what the fuck they're talking about."

"You have —" he began.

I cut him off. "If I didn't have children, I wouldn't believe I'd ever met her."

He looked at me. "I won't argue with your feelings," he said.

"Thank you."

"But you were married to a brilliant woman for —"

"The past doesn't exist, Scott."

"Time goes by fast, much too fast. I understand that. But it was at least fifty years and you know those were good years."

"The past doesn't exist. Haven't you noticed? It's gone. That's why we call it the past. It's not real anymore."

"What you had with Alba —"

"It has no more reality than a wish," I told him. "It's a romantic fiction."

He started to speak but changed his mind, shutting his mouth so abruptly I heard his teeth snap together. Looking back, I see that Scott was remarkably patient with me, for he believed wholly in reason and I was clearly mindless. His father had been a linotype operator for a Boston newspaper, his mother a Trotskyite and later a worker for the Democratic Party, and Scott had grown up a secular humanist — "a tribe without a God," he liked to say. Scott was a good guy.

❦

It was strange to live alone, to embrace no one and to have no one put her arms around me, and sometimes it felt like my nerves were on the outside, aching to be soothed, or inside like it was thirst. But it wasn't thirst or pain, it was loneliness. Lucy Dolan who had done babysitting for us was now in her mid-fifties but still slender and straight, and at Vanderzee's exhibit she had given me a tight warm hug that lingered, the way vibrations linger after you strike the nerve strings.

❦

I liked Shannon. I'd buy a cup of coffee, then stand under the leaky awning to watch the cars going by in the rain and talk with her between customers. She showed me she had moved her wedding ring to her right hand. "Because if I keep it where it was, people will think I'm married to Fitz and I don't want anybody to think that. I wanted to keep wearing it on my left hand at least, but it only fits my ring finger, so I had to move it to my other hand."

I told her I never had a wedding ring, but hers was beautiful, I said.

"Yeah, I know," Shannon said. "I told him not to waste the money but he insisted. The emeralds make it different."

"My wife's ring is in a little velvet bag on her bureau.

I never knew her fingers were so slender. It's a small plain gold ring. That's all. With our initials inside."

"I have a friend whose husband died last year and she wears his ring on a necklace chain," Shannon said.

"That's something."

"It hangs down, you know, so it's over her heart."

When I got home I looked through Alba's jewelry and found a silver chain and put her ring on the chain and wore it. It hangs down to my breastbone. It's comforting and whenever I want I can touch it.

❦

Before sunset I always go for a walk the way we used to at that gentle hour. It's a roundabout walk and halfway along it crosses through a field with a creek and a margin of tall grass where redwing blackbirds nest and wild flowers grow, and eventually the path goes beside Franklin's Four Seasons, the flower nursery. Alba always took an interest in what was blossoming in the greenhouses. Then the path rises up a little slope to where we would have to lift the branches of a birch and duck under to go out the street and so to the road where we lived. Now I would remember how sometimes her hair would catch on those branches and I tried to recall just how her dress would swing as she stepped ahead. If she was here with me on these walks, all those times — and she was, she was — then I don't understand how she cannot be. You cannot be at one moment and then not be at the next.

❦

Q. What is man?

A. Man is a creature composed of body and soul, and made to the image and likeness of God.

Q. Is this likeness in the body or in the soul?

A. This likeness is chiefly in the soul.

Q. How is the soul like to God?

A. The soul is like to God because it is a spirit that will never die, and has understanding and free will.

I understood all that. I knew what my body was and what my mind was and my personality and my character, but I didn't know what my soul was and I began to wonder about that. One day I was watching my father work on a grave marker, a rare artistic job that only he and none of the two or three workers he hired could do, because it had a butterfly carved at the top and a border of pomegranates to the left and right of the inscription, old symbols of resurrection. After a while, I asked him what the soul was. He removed his safety glasses and rubbed the two pink indents that the glasses had pinched on the bridge of his nose. He smiled a bit. "I think that's a question for your mother." I told him I had already asked her. He hesitated, then said, "Well, there's your uncle Zitti. He talks about his soul as easily as other men talk about their digestion." He put on his safety glasses and took up the chisel again, then turned to me. "Or you could ask your uncle Nicolo," he added. "He has opinions about the soul, too."

Uncle Nicolo had a big book with illustrations by Gustave Doré which Nick and I used to take from the bookcase and open on the floor to look at — dark and frightening scenes, like those naked men trapped in the ice of a frozen lake, one man gnawing on the bald head of another, or that naked woman who was twisted around, pulling out her own hair. Those were the damned being tortured forever in Hell, which was the first part of Dante's long poem. The second part was Purgatory where people got horribly punished, but after doing penance for their sins they were admitted into Paradise, which was the third part of the poem. The pictures of Hell were the ones we looked at most, because they were so gruesome and because everyone was naked there, unlike in Paradise where the souls wore clothes. The souls were really souls and not bodies, but Gustave Doré drew the bodies to show how the souls in Hell felt horrible pain forever, which Nick and I thought was terribly unfair of God, because forever was way too long a time even if they had sinned when they had been alive, but it did give you an idea of how cruel God could be when he wanted.

A few years later, Nick said he didn't believe in souls. We were walking with Veronica, coming back from the field where Sandro used to fly his hawk and where Dante and Mercurio used to shoot, but now uncle Nicolo had a Victory Garden there because of the war.

We were crossing the old burying ground when Nick announced, "Frankly, I don't believe in souls." Maybe that was because his father was an aeronautical engineer at MIT and didn't believe much in religion. But Veronica said she was sure we had souls. "We have understanding and free will, which is what the soul has, and the part of us that has understanding and free will, that's the soul part." She smiled, waiting for us to see how clear and obvious it was, but I still wasn't sure if I believed in souls or not.

Nick said, "Oh, no. Because if you believe in a soul you have to believe in heaven and hell, and maybe heaven is all right, but what about hell? Do you really truly believe in hell?"

Veronica didn't answer and we walked along and climbed over the low stone wall into the backyard. "So what if there's a hell," she said lightly. "Nobody actually goes there anymore."

❦

Some days when Shannon wasn't at the Barista stand I'd swing around to the Daily Grind to see Gordon and we'd talk about the strangeness of life or what was wrong with politicians or the Red Sox, but today he talked mostly about whether he should look for a shop with more floor space. He missed the old place in Boston, which was larger, but he liked Lexington "because this town is full of intellectuals who drink coffee all day." Here he was on the main street, but if he moved to a bigger place it would be farther from the center of town. On the other hand, if he had more floor space he could serve more people and sell more Rancilio espresso machines — but there was a lot to be said for staying in the same place, because the Daily Grind, having been here ten years, "now these fussy people know where to come to buy Hawaiian Kona or Monsoon Malabar." So Gordon went from this side to that side, debating with himself while we worked on the ancient coffee roaster, until eventually it was fixed and I held the fancy front end while he bolted it back into place. We must have talked an hour, and all that time I was able to forget who I was.

❦

It betrays Alba to say she has died or she is dead and I say it only because that's what people can understand. I believe Alba will never die, that she has understanding and free will, and that she knows me. I would like to die and be united with her forever, the way we were. I don't know what I believe.

❦

I drove to La Pâtisserie and bought two plain croissants, just so I could have twelve minutes of bright chat at the pastry case with Katelin (twenty-five, welcoming smile, warm white arms, and a flower in her hair), but she could not rescue me so I drove away, ashamed of myself, to Café Mondello to buy a latte so I could chat up Felicia (twenty-one, blue jeans and a tight white top with a blue dab of shadow under each nipple), after which I drove home, horribly alone and feeling like shit. I do things like that every day.

🦢

One time I was having lunch with Scott and he asked what I was doing these days, and I said, "Not much, really."

"Have you been painting?"

"No. No painting."

He nodded, as if in agreement with me. "It's too early. You need more time. A little more time."

"What's the point?"

"What do you mean?" he asked.

"I mean, what's the purpose of all this — all this living, this going on? I really don't understand. I'm serious. What's the point?"

"That's a rather large question. Whole philosophies have been built —"

I cut him off. "It's not a philosophical question for me. It's in my guts. I don't understand what the fuck I'm doing here. Why am I doing whatever I do? I ask myself that every shitty day. *What's the goddamn point?*"

Scott shifted uneasily in his chair, then he looks at me a moment and says, "Did you enjoy your sandwich? Your half-sandwich, I mean."

"I guess so, yes."

"Were you enjoying our conversation?"

"Yes, sure."

"That's the point."

"*That's* the point?"

"Yes."

❦

I drifted from room to room (nothing out of place, the books in a row, the pillows smooth, the empty chairs at a conversational angle) and I realized I'm the ghost haunting this house — I'm dead and Alba is alive and this world is an illusion I have because I'm dead.

❦

Danae and Chiara will be away at college soon, so before they go they came here to be with their grandfather for the day — you're right, Alba, we're fortunate to have such grandchildren. We were driving on Great Meadow Road after a shower when we saw a big rainbow and of course they wanted to take pictures of it, so I pulled into the parking lot at the playing fields and they took phone photos. The rainbow was large and seemed to hang in the air above the faraway soccer fields and I kept wishing I had my camera so I could send you a photo of it. That's what I mean by crazy.

❦

It's a privilege to love someone and I loved Alba. "I'm so happy you found me," she used to say. I was handsome, her man from the sea, and the one she loved best in the whole world. She's gone, so I'm not handsome anymore. I'm an old man driving home with a pizza and I'm sobbing because some cheerful asshole is singing on the radio about his love who is gone beyond the sea and the moon and stars, but she's waiting and watching for him, and someday he'll find her there on the shore and they'll be together and he'll embrace her, just as he did before. When the song was over I stopped sniveling, blew my nose, drove back onto the road and got home in one piece.

🐝

Can you follow this goddamn story? I know it's a jumbled mess but it's what I can recall, and also some notes I wrote to Alba, plus unconnected pieces. Parts are missing and some of them may be important, but they're missing because I don't remember, or because I do remember and don't want to. I want to write about that first year, though I don't know why I want to do even that much. I'm blundering ahead, like our moronic blundering Creator.

🐝

I had figured Shannon to be forty years old — it turned out she was only thirty-three, younger than my kids and not way older than my grandkids, but her getting kicked around had added another seven years to her face. Her father owned The Copper Kettle in Charlestown and Shannon liked to brag she had grown up in a bar. Her father died when she was thirteen. When she was sixteen and pregnant she came home from school one day to find her clothes and the other ten things she owned had been dumped in a cardboard box outside the back door, which is what her mother had always threatened to do. Her mother, who used to call Shannon *The Disgrace*, died about five years ago, refusing to allow Shannon into her hospice room. Shannon dropped out of high school to have the baby and never went back, so she has that seventeen-year-old daughter, plus a teenage son from a later marriage — he's living with his father — and a daughter Robert brought with him when they married. Fitzpatrick, the guy living with her now, has a son and daughter he visits every other weekend. Fitz's ex is a bitch, Shannon tells me. "He's got hardly no money left to live on. I can't pay my rent. That's why we're living together," she says. "Pooling resources."

"It's only a matter of money?" I asked her.

"You mean do I love him? No. — Oh, the sex is good, very good, but I don't love him. How could I?"

$$\mathcal{S}$$

When I go for a walk, nobody knows where I am. Together or not, Alba knew where I was and I knew where she was. Now I walk down this street and then around the corner and then along a ways and then across the field of brown grass and dried stalks where the wild flowers grew, then beside the old Franklin place and their deserted greenhouses, some of the glass busted, and up to the street. Nobody knows where I am. I've vanished. I can press my hand hard against my parka, press against my chest until I feel Alba's wedding ring in my flesh. That's our secret. My eyes are watery and I don't know if it's the icy wind or my thoughts, but no one's around and anyway it doesn't matter. If I could slip quietly away, that would be good. My hands are cold and the sunset colorless and I'm here walking by myself or maybe I'm gone.

※

A letter from Leo Conti arrived, actually not a letter but a sheet from a real-estate agent's book of available properties. It displayed a big lousy color photo of a brownstone building on Newbury Street and a list of the building's basic specifications. On the back of the sheet Leo had written, *What do you think?* Only Leo and his crooked guardian angel know why he sent it to me. Newbury was one of the most expensive streets in the country. What did I think about what? Had he bought the whole damn building? Had he signed a lease for one rotten floor? Was he trying to make up his mind about where to move his gallery? I crumpled the paper and lobbed it into the kitchen wastebasket. I sent Leo a one-word postcard — *Excellent!* — which I figured would make him happy.

❦

Nils Petersen and Hanna had returned from the Netherlands and now the DeCordova was showing some of Nils' work in an exhibit of artists' books — which is when an artist, such as Nils, makes a book out of folded paper or sheet metal or, for that matter, crispy toast, or takes a regular book and does things to it. I was happy he was making artists' books and no longer producing computer art, which I've always believed is shit without the smell. Of course, writers say that artists' books are just another way to destroy the printed word, but writers are born complaining, and at least these things are made by hand to live and die in this world, not cyberspace. Avalon and Sebastian were going, so I went with them. It was good to be with Hanna and Nils again and to have a relaxed conversation about one thing and another. Scott was there with his wife Rachel, which was good, because she has wandering pains and tends to get desperately anxious when she leaves the house. Vanderzee came with Gail and Winona, and eleven-year-old Saskia. Scott and I talked for a while and set up a lunch date at a new place called Fête Champêtre, which he said had good food despite the rococo name. And other friends and acquaintances turned up, like Barbabianco and his wife, then Tom Hay and his wife, and George Agathos and his wife, but I was getting more and more aware of

Renato without his wife, so I was grateful when Avalon and Sebastian said they were ready to leave.

☙

I carved a jack-o'-lantern for Halloween, filled a bowl with small candies, and let the neighborhood kids take however much they wanted while their parents stood at the edge of the road with flashlights, calling a cheerful, "Thank you!" as they all trooped away. Clearly, I'm learning to do things without thinking, which is good. A while later, I hauled the trash barrel out, big stupid Orion overhead, meaning it's going to get colder and darker for longer and longer.

☙

"But what is the purpose of life?" uncle Zitti asked. That was at Thanksgiving at his house in 1949. He was back from a trip to Italy where he had taken care of his mother's property, for she had died that summer and maybe the visit to the graves of his mother and father had brought those thoughts to mind. "We're so busy living, we don't think about that," he said.

I caught the scent of Veronica's lily-of-the-valley perfume and felt her warm breath on my ear as she whispered, Here comes some philosophy.

We were a dozen people and dinner was finished, but no one had left the table — the glossy white linen was a disordered landscape of forgotten forks, nutcrackers, rumpled napkins, dessert bowls, chestnuts, ropes of dried figs, broken walnut shells, and those little paper boxes that Torrone came in, boxes with old-fashioned portraits of famous Italians. Three or four conversations were crisscrossing at once while everyone had another of cup of coffee or another glass of wine. Zitti, who had been born in the Abruzzi and brought to this country by his parents when he was thirteen, was saying, "The top of the church tower was shot away and the *municipio* — you know, the mayor's building, across the square from the church — it looked like it had been used for target practice. Other than that, no change. Even the smells were the same." He smiled, remembering the smells. Then he must have thought again of his mother, his face somber once more. He sighed and said, "I should have gone back a year earlier."

Aunt Candida, his wife, said, "Zitti, please! How could you have known? They could have told you. *Ma ne anche una parola.* She could have written."

"Life —" Zitti began, then hesitated.

"It doesn't do any good to blame yourself," Candida told him, leaving to answer the phone that had begun to ring.

My father had put two walnuts in his palm and now he gently and carefully closed his fist, cracking them but not crushing them. He wasn't engaged in the conversation, because his mother and father had died when he was nineteen and death didn't interest him.

Candida returned, telling us that Mercurio said he'd be here in time for dessert. Uncle Zitti glanced at her without saying that we'd already finished dessert, and she replied, "There's still some pumpkin pie and spumoni."

"I wonder if Coral will be coming with him," my mother said.

We all knew that Mercurio and Coral weren't getting along.

"I didn't dare ask," Candida said.

My father opened his hand and began to pick out the pieces of shattered shell.

"This French philosopher, Albert Camus, he thinks life is absurd," Zitti said. "Absurd and with no purpose."

"We make up purposes as we go along," Nicolo said. "We keep changing the purpose, but the important thing is to have a purpose, a goal. Making progress toward our goal give us pleasure, and as soon as we get there, we discover another goal, further ahead."

Aunt Marissa, his wife, said, "Always going and never arriving. I don't know if that's so good."

"The purpose of life is to work," my father declared. "Work saves more souls than Jesus."

Zitti continued, "Camus says that death makes life absurd and pointless."

"You think your mother's life was pointless?" Candida asked him.

"I didn't say that. We're talking about Camus' beliefs, not mine."

"Camus is absurd," Candida murmured.

"Maybe the poor man has no family life," my mother suggested.

Zitti shrugged and opened his hands, palms up, to show he didn't know what to make of any of this. "Or maybe he says those things simply because he's French."

"You detest the French," Veronica said. "So why do you make me take French if you feel that way?"

Zitti looked at her a moment, clearly surprised. "The purpose of life is to have children," he announced to us. "That's the goal." He smiled and glanced around the table. "And we're all doing very well. *In vino veritas!*" he said, raising his empty glass. "Is there any left in that bottle or should I get another?"

Nick, across the table from me, gave me a look and tilted his head toward the door, suggesting we could escape. Veronica's brother Jason and my brother Bart had already been excused, but we were older and had to stay longer. I drained the wine from my glass and then pushed my chair back from the table.

"Where are you going?" Veronica whispered, pinching my arm.

"We're going upstairs to tear the dresses off your dolls and play doctor," I whispered. "Like we used to."

Veronica spoke up. "Can we be excused?" she asked, speaking to no one in particular.

"Take some dishes into the kitchen when you go," Candida told her.

Veronica chose the platter of turkey bones from the

sideboard. Nick and I picked up our coffee cups, wine-glasses, loose silverware. We three went to the jumbled kitchen, dropped everything into the crowded sink and went out the door to the backyard. The sky was a clean light blue and the air was chilly. Bart and Jason were tossing a basketball at the hoop over the garage door. Nick took out a pack of cigarettes, offered me one. "What about me?" Veronica said.

Nick laughed. "You're too young. It will stunt your growth," he said.

"I smoke all the time," she retorted.

"Oh, sure," I said.

"Let me take a puff," she said.

So I give her my cigarette and let her have a few puffs. We three walked around to the front and sat on the steps in the sun.

"I miss Nanna and Nonno's big house," Veronica said. "I liked how everybody used to go there when we were kids. I miss that."

"Nonno had to sell it," Nick said. "He had no money left after the war."

"I might go visit Nanna in the villa in Palermo," Veronica said.

"I bet Mercurio drives up without Coral," Nick said.

"I bet he drives up in his red MG," I said.

"Let me have another puff on your cigarette," Veronica said.

I had never wondered what the purpose of life was and for a while after that Thanksgiving dinner, whenever I did think about it, I figured that you lived life and that was all there was to it. Uncle Zitti's questions were puzzlers and often confusing, but uncle Nicolo's answers were understandable, like common sense. Zitti told me more than once that the unexamined life isn't worth living but I was nineteen and, the way I looked at it, you couldn't examine life and live it at the same time. I was taking courses at the School of the Museum of Fine Arts and living in Boston, in Back Bay, in my own room and on my own, and I was meeting women, not fourteen-year-old kids like Alba, and I was painting like crazy, so there was no time to examine life — that was something you might do later, maybe when you were forty years old and getting philosophical. I was living it and that's the way I liked it.

❦

I see I haven't properly introduced those two uncles, or even my father, so I'll do that now. Zitti and Nicolo and my father Fidèle married three Cavallù sisters — Zitti to Candida, Nicolo to Marisa, and my father to Bianca. My father, Nicolo, and Zitti had happy marriages and enjoyed each other's company. Nicolo, a calm and gentle man, had a head as bald as the dome at MIT where he was a professor of aeronautical engineering. He was also an amateur balloonist and the author of a book on electronic orbits (highly regarded when it was published), which was rendered obsolete by quantum mechanics a year later. As a kid working in his father's grocery store, he kept Volume 1 of the 1889 edition of the *Encyclopædia Britannica* under the counter to read between customers. Zitti, a lively man with sparkling eyes, always about to break into a smile, was a professor of philosophy, inventor of an onomatopoetic language, and author of the epic poem *Luna*, about a voyage on the moon through those dark seas discovered by Galileo. As an immigrant kid, one of his jobs was to climb down into railroad tank cars with a hose and a scrub brush to wash the inside. My father, who for no particular reason would sing Puccini, or kiss my mother's cheek and pat her behind, had begun in 1920 the college education he longed for, but that same year his father and mother perished in the Influenza Epidemic. He took on his father's uncompleted masonry jobs, then kept at the work to support himself and his younger sister, became a skilled worker in stone, tile and mosaic, and an avid reader.

Those two uncles had opposing ideas about everything, including education, so when I enrolled in the Museum School they began to send me books and reading lists. From Nicolo, I still have Watts and Rule's lovely little book *Descriptive Geometry*, and Sears' *Principles of Physics*, and from Zitti, Ovid's *Metamorphoses* in Latin, plus a translation made by Arthur Golding in 1567, and a paperback edition of Castiglione's *The Book of the Courtier*. The Courtier's ideal man was athletic and bold, but even-tempered and equally good at conversation, horsemanship and poetry, so the book was a useful and practical guide, my uncle insisted, though I doubted anything written in the sixteenth century could help me much. Above all, I should strive for the Courtier's "*sprezzatura*," a wonderful word, uncle Zitti told me, that means exactly what it sounds like — nonchalance, spirit and grace, making hard things look easy. I've failed at that, too.

❦

I walked out for a cup of coffee with the sky gray as ice on one side and already black on the other. In the cold I keep up a good pace, better than most people my age. My mother's great-grandfather was born with the hindquarters of a horse and though I'm adopted it's possible one of his rash animalistic progeny fathered me, which would be why I was left on that doorstep and why I have these legs. Alba always liked those family stories but now she's gone, so the stories don't make sense anymore. The trees are empty, exposing the bare houses. One of the shutters on the empty Franklin house is hanging upside down from the bottom hinge. I'm walking to a cup of coffee even though it will taste like yesterday's piss, so I should admit to myself that I'm going there simply to be around people but, to show I'm not a lonely old man, I'll leave after twenty minutes. Then comes the bleak walk home in the dark and I'll wonder again what the hell I'm doing here, walking alone and to where and what for.

I bumped into Lucy Dolan in Cambridge in front of a delicatessen, so we went in and had lunch. She looked very good, maybe because of her bright quilted jacket and scarf, or maybe because the cold made her cheeks glow. She had come from a store auction, hoping to buy second-hand equipment for the bakery she planned to open

"Everything costs more than I can afford," she said, almost laughing. "And I mean the second-hand stuff — the new equipment is beyond-belief expensive."

I asked where she planned to have her shop.

"That's the other thing that's expensive, floor space. I want to be near Boston, but rents are so high I have to look farther and farther away. I've been asking Meg for advice. She's had that shop for years. Right now I'm living at my friend Alison's and I dread the thought of having to move from the city. — I prefer people to cows and trees," she added.

We talked about city life and country life and Lucy told me about her daughter, Jenny, who had found a job as a technical writer. "She majored in Environmental Science but she's a technical writer for a bioengineering company. I suppose she's lucky to have any kind of job in this economy." We agreed the economy was lousy and that the rich got richer and the poor got poorer, then we ordered lunch, talked about the small-size shop she was looking for, and when our sandwiches arrived she asked was I painting.

"I don't feel like painting."

"You should. You're really good at it."

I said thank you.

"I don't mean you should paint if you don't want to," she emended. "I mean, you're good at it and it would be great if you did feel like painting." She hesitated. "It must be terrible. I mean, she was —" She broke off. "How are you?" she asked.

"I'm all right. I wish I didn't cry so much."

"I cry at least five times a week."

"Oh? What's going on in your life?" I asked.

"No, no," she said, touching my wrist reassuringly. "I'm really all right. After working fifteen years in somebody else's bakery I'm about to open my own shop and everything's too damned expensive. But I had a double major, English and Classics, so I'm prepared." She laughed. "Now tell me about Skye and Astrid and Brizio and what they're doing."

So I told her about my children and we talked and talked and she told me about San Francisco and Monterey ("Nobody thinks very hard out there. Everything's on the back burner. I may be baking bread, but I still like to read and think about things.") and about her marriage ("It wasn't toxic like some I've seen. We just got worn down until nothing was left. Maybe it was my baby being born and dying the next day, maybe it was Jenny with colic when we lived in a one-room cabin, or maybe it was Alaska or his job, or maybe it was me.") and about Jacob Bergstrom, the only father she knew ("It was easy enough for me to choose him, but amazing that he could he be so caring to somebody else's twelve-year-old kid.")

I confess that all the while she talked, I saw how good she looked, neither young nor old despite the finely etched lies around her eyes, and when she laughed it was dazzling.

Jacob — she always called him by his first name — was her mother's second husband, the wedding taking place when Lucy was five years old. Then one day in June when Lucy was twelve, her mother took her on a long automobile ride to Saratoga, in Upstate New York, where she had already secured a job on a newspaper, and she explained to Lucy that they were going to live in Saratoga from now on because Jacob was a loser, just like Lucy's father had been — and besides, her mother's old college friend from years ago lived in nearby Albany and he would be nice to them. Lucy lived with her mother in Saratoga that summer, but in September, when school was about to begin, Lucy bought a bus ticket to Albany, and from Albany she bought another to Springfield, halfway across Massachusetts, which used up almost all the money she had. She phoned Jacob from Springfield and told him she was coming home but had run out of money and could he please come and get her at the Greyhound bus station, so he drove to the bus station in Springfield and brought her back to his house, her bedroom, and her school friends. We never knew what the legal arrangements were, but Lucy, who began to spell her name Luci, grew up as Jacob Bergstrom's daughter and when she was a junior in high school we asked Luci, or Lucia Bergstrom as she then called herself, to do babysitting for us. As for Jacob, he was knocked down by a brain hemorrhage while at his desk in the cataloging department of the North Shore Library, shortly after Lucy had started her senior year in college, so she returned home to take care of him until he died nine months later.

Now as we got ready to leave the delicatessen, we were talking again about her bakery shop and pies or cookies or other delicacies, and I was raving about Italian pastries, throwing my hands around, when she caught me by my wrist and laughed and said, "If I tied your hands you wouldn't be able to say a word, you're so Italian."

"Sicilian, actually," I said, knowing only how warm her hand was.

❦

I woke up having a wet dream about Susan Salter, or what passes for a wet dream at eighty-something. I hardly know the woman. She was Alba's colleague, not mine — bright, vivacious, and lots of jingling bracelets — so here she is rolling me onto my back and getting into the saddle. Wide awake now, just me and not much to mop up, almost nothing at all. I shaved and showered and was thinking of Alba and how she could explain me in a way that made sense, which is what I desperately need when I'm this confused.

☙

I should go back and write more about Fletcher and Katherine. Kate teaches literature at a community college and Fletch is a surrealist poet, if that means anything, a part-time novelist and the owner-editor of Prospero's Books, a small press that turns out maybe three books a year. I've never asked how they survive. They live in a three-story house with a wraparound porch and a jumble of rooms, some bedrooms, of course, but others with sports equipment and old-fashioned bookbinding gear or musical instruments, and a carriage house out back with cartons of books, and a tree house which must have been fun for their kids who are now grown up and have kids of their own. During one of those numb days after Alba was gone, Fletch brought me his wooden clamps and we repaired a chair. It took all my effort to focus on what we were doing as my vision shrank to a small circle no bigger than my two hands and there was a continuous rushing sound in my head. They invited me to dinner one evening, the three of us dining on soup and thick bread in their warm kitchen. It was a comfort and at the same time painful, because Fletch and Kate were our age and deeply enjoyed each other's company — I mean, I returned to this empty house and drifted from room to room, pulling down the shades until I was back in the kitchen, feeling lower than whale shit and stupidly puzzled that Alba wasn't here anymore.

❦

I told Shannon I'd have an espresso. She began banging coffee grounds out of the portafilter (angrily, I thought) and told me — BANG! BANG! — she was pissed because she had to sell her pickup truck, because her grandfather needed round-the-clock — BANG! BANG! — care.

"Round-the-clock is expensive," I said.

"It's fuckin' impossible," Shannon said. "He doesn't want to leave his home. He's seventy-eight. What can you do?"

I shrugged and told her I could understand her grandfather feeling that way.

"We were keeping the truck like money in the bank," Shannon said. "It was like savings. When I sell the truck we'll have nothing left. It's a good vehicle. It was one of our best things. You want spice cake with this?"

"Not this time."

"A red Nissan Titan with 110,000 miles on it," she continued. "Robert bought it new, for work, and we went everywhere in it, down the Cape and up to Montreal. I still keep his tools and things in it." Then she went silent and attended to my coffee, her face closed. "I like the way it smells," she added. "You get inside and slam the door and you feel like going places." She gave me the little espresso cup which I held in both hands to warm my fingers. "If I don't take care of my grandfather, who will? No one, that's who," she said.

☙

My kids were coming with their families for the Christmas holidays, so I did what they asked me to do. I got a tree, and the giant who owns the farm down the road helped me set it upright in the stand. The next morning I climbed into the attic and brought down the boxes and big cartons of Christmas gear that Alba and I had wrapped and put away a year ago. That evening I strung the lights and hung all the sparkling ornaments, even those little gold balls that we got for our first little tree, though the paint was flaking away from inside the glass and we hadn't used them for years. When I had finished hanging the last of the icicles, I turned off the living room lamps, and in the dark I turned on the tree lights. And here's Renato, gathering up the empty boxes and sobbing, stumbling over a carton and landing on the sofa to bawl, because it had been so hard to do all this all alone, and now the tree is so beautiful, soft and quiet, but still Alba hasn't come back.

☙

They came for Christmas week, one family at a time. Our Skye and her husband Eric, the perpetually displaced Canadian anthropologist, and their five kids, ranging from nine to twenty-one, came two days before Christmas, and stayed most of the day after Christmas in order to be here when our Brizio — Fabrizio on the birth certificate — and his wife Heather, a true Abenaki without an Abenaki name, arrived with their two boys. Brizio and his family stayed until our Astrid — who persists in calling herself Galaxy in the credits of her documentaries — and her husband Weston and their two kids arrived the day before New Year's Eve, so some family was here through January first. One of our secret pleasures was to be in the next room, fixing this or adjusting that, but all the while listening to our children in the kitchen catching up with each other, talking a mile a minute, laughing and gossiping. Alba and I, we'd exchange a glance, that's all.

❦

Denise, an old friend from when I was single, had married and moved to France, sending us a yearly Christmas card with notes about herself, her husband and their two children. Her husband had died half a year before Alba. When she received the news about Alba, she phoned and we had a good talk. This Christmas her card arrived in January — *Dear Renato, I'm sorry to say the second year isn't any easier than the first, no matter what people tell you. But the children & grandchildren are well. Love, Denise.*

❦

Around sunset the wind stopped, leaving the snow packed hard, the top flat and smooth as a sheet of fine-tooth paper. I got into my parka and went out to shovel, but first checked my watch because no one was going to call from the door — *Renato, you've worked long enough. I've made hot chocolate!* I had a phone in my coat pocket, in case my heart jammed but left me enough time to gasp for help. The air was like ice, like that first scent of ether before you go under. I shoveled a path from the front door to my car, which I had parked farther down the driveway so I'd have a shorter distance to shovel between the car and the road. When I checked my watch again I was huffing and puffing, so I didn't get to the road. I went in, pulled off my gear, made a mug of hot cocoa for myself and sat at the kitchen table. The window reflected like a black mirror, as if I was outside seeing myself sitting alone, all alone in the lighted kitchen, so I turned off the light and my reflection mercifully disappeared. Now I could see the shed and the smooth snow all the way down to the black woods. I sat in the dark, drinking the cocoa and looking out at the snow and the woods. I wasn't thinking of Alba, or maybe I was, but anyway it felt like tears were coming, so I pulled down the window shade and turned on the light. I didn't know what to do. I went looking through the bookcase for something to read and saw one of my sketchbooks, so I took it back to the kitchen and did a line drawing of the cocoa mug and the place mat with the short fringe. It was a pretty good drawing.

❧

I thought the album cover for *Sgt. Pepper's Lonely Hearts Club Band* was crappy art. My cousin Nick said it was a joke, all those black-and-white pop-photo faces dolled up like waxworks (I still thought it was crappy) and Veronica said the music was the important thing, not the album cover, said her kids liked the music even if they were too young to understand it, and Nick's wife Maeve said that for the first time in her life she was listening to rock and enjoying it, and not only the Beatles — which was what Alba had said five minutes ago. We were sitting on the grass by the old workshop where the faded sign still said *Stillamare's Cut Stone & Tile Company*, because my father continued to cut stone for special jobs. My father and uncle Nicolo and uncle Zitti were playing bocce. Nonno had a bocce court of fine blue gravel, but my father's was good, too, this long flat stretch of grass framed by weathered gray boards laid on their long edges. The balls were the old kind, made of wood, not plastic, so they made the satisfying, familiar *clack* sound when knocked together. It was a warm and drowsy afternoon, the air absolutely still. We had fallen silent, watching them play. Then Nick said, "We've been watching them play this same game for over twenty-five years." Then he lay back with his hands folded under his head and looked up into the tree.

"Don't be rude," Veronica told him. "We hardly ever get together and I like seeing everyone together. And it's never the same game." She shaded her eyes with her hand and watched them play.

"I'm not being rude," Nick said, closing his eyes. "I'm just saying we've watched our fathers play *bocce* for twenty-five years. And in a while my father and your father will talk politics or the meaning of meaning, and they'll ask Renato's father to decide some fine point they can't agree on." He kept his eyes closed.

"If they agreed, they wouldn't have anything to talk about," Maeve said.

At that moment, Zitti and Nicolo were watching while my father was crouched over the pallino, deciding whose ball was closest by sliding two twigs together, side-by-side, until they fit exactly between the pallino and one of the closest balls. Then, holding the twigs fixed, he tested to see if they'd fit or not between the pallino and the other close ball.

"They agree about Vietnam, anyway," Nick said.

Bennett, Veronica's husband, murmured, "Vietnam." He was lying with his eyes shut and his hands folded on his chest and I thought he had fallen asleep, but he was so political he could probably say Vietnam in his sleep.

"It's a beautiful day — why are the kids indoors?" Maeve said.

"Don't ask me," Alba said. "I'm enjoying the heat and not thinking."

Veronica stood up, brushing some stray grass from her dress. "I'm going in to help with the coffee and things." Alba and Maeve got to their feet, saying, "Wait, wait."

Nick sat up and opened his eyes. "The shade from this tree keeps moving away," he informed me. "Can't you do something about that?"

When the bocce game ended we were offered a choice of spumoni or lemon sherbet — that was cried out by Veronica from the kitchen window — along with our coffee and pasticceria. Uncle Zitti and aunt Candida and uncle Nicolo and aunt Marissa gathered the little kids and sat with them at the old plank table under the big maple where my dad and his two or three workmen used to eat their lunch in the summer. The rest of us were sitting on the grass but, naturally, the kids kept wandering from the table to wherever they wanted to go. Alba came carrying a tray with the ice cream and sherbet — a beautiful young woman in a white dress, the top part close-fitting and the bottom part long and flowing. I had lemon sherbet, tart and finely textured with vanishing ice crystals, while Alba chose the spumoni. Later, somebody passed me a plate of Italian cookies which my mother must have bought at a specialty store. "How can you tell if these are stale or not?" I asked.

"Renato," Alba said, a rebuke in her voice that only I could hear.

"All I mean is that they're born hard and taste dry from birth," I told her.

"Oh, is *that* all you mean," she said lightly.

"The French are good at pastry, the Italians are good at the main meal," Nick said.

"Cannoli are as good as anything the French make," Veronica said. "And sfogliatelle, too."

"This would be a nice day to pass a joint around," Nick said.

Bennett suddenly looked alert, even cheerful. "I have some weed in the car."

"He wants to get us arrested," Veronica said. "He thinks pot smoking is a political act. Like long hair."

"Who wants to play bocce?" Nick asked, getting up.

Nick and Bennett drifted off to play bocce, trailed by Maeve and Veronica, and I went to the table to refill my coffee cup. Uncle Zitti was talking about the Big Bang theory. Uncle Nicolo said it wasn't a theory anymore, but a fact. "They've found all that background radiation and it's everywhere," he said. "It's exactly what they predicted would be left after the Creation."

"I like the Steady State theory better," Zitti said. "I like the idea of a universe that always was and always will be, an eternal universe. Like God in the catechism," he added.

"Well, Steady State theory's gone," Nicolo told him. "Now it's all Big Bang and cosmic expansion. In fact, they calculate how fast the universe is expanding, then run the numbers backward to find when it began."

"That would be a Monday," my father said cheerfully. "The beginning took seven days and was complete by Sunday, so if you run the numbers backward it begins on Monday. I love reasoning this way. Ask me another."

"Ah, numbers," Zitti said and heaved a sigh. "People have too much faith in numbers."

"The language of nature is written with numbers," Nicolo told him. "Galileo thought so."

"And Saint Augustine believed God created the universe with a word," said Zitti.

I said, "I thought you men settled these questions thirty years ago."

Zitti smiled. "We know more now than we did thirty years ago," he said. "We can *really* settle things now."

"We're wiser," Nicolo said. "We're wise old men."

"Older, that's for sure," my father said.

"Did Augustine have anything to say about atoms?" Nicolo asked. "Atoms are getting very strange. They smash them open and all these subatomic particles fly out, like a clock with too many parts."

"No, Augustine had nothing to say about atoms," Zitti said. "That was Lucretius. Did you ever get around to reading Lucretius?" he asked me.

Lucretius was on one of the reading lists my uncle had given me years ago when I left home for art school. "I began it," I said.

"I've never read Lucretius, that's for damn sure," my father said.

"He believed in atoms and only in atoms," Zitti said. "A materialist. But brilliant."

"I thought that was Democritus," my father said, his voice vague as he searched his memory. "You know, Blake has a little poem about that. I've always liked Blake. — The atoms of Democritus and Newton's particles of light, and so forth."

"Right, Lucretius was a follower of Democritus," Zitti continued. "Said everything was composed of atoms and everything, sooner or later, dispersed back to atoms scattered through the void. He said the gods weren't interested in humans and didn't create them or anything else. Just atoms hooking onto each other, then falling apart. That's Lucretius."

" 'The atoms of Democritus and Newton's particles of light, are sands upon the Red Sea shore, where Israel's tents do shine so bright' — that's it," my father said, pleased.

Alba had come out the door with Skye. "Ren," she called to me. "Did we bring a camera?"

"I didn't," I said, putting down my coffee. "Want to go for a walk?"

Behind me, Nicolo was saying that the Red Sox were looking amazingly good this summer.

We walked down past the old grape arbor — the frame made of iron pipe almost forty years ago — the vines as thick as your arm and dense with leaves, and past the vegetable garden, sadly limited now to a dozen tomato plants and a couple of rows of garlic and peppers, then around to the remnants of the ancient canal and back up past the barn to where the others were lying or sitting on the grass in the shade of the old maple. "It's a beautiful day," Alba remarked. "Una bella giornata, like your mother says."

❧

Yes, we made love for the first time when Alba was fourteen and I was seventeen, and at the end of summer she went back to high school and I went off to the School of the Museum of Fine Arts and we thought that was the end of it. But one winter day we bumped into each other on a sidewalk in Boston — by then she was a student at Boston University — and a couple of years later we discovered each other at a sweltering outdoor party in the West End where she was drinking straight gin, and before leaving I looked for her and found she was throwing up in the bushes, so I went off with somebody else. It was maybe two or three years afterward I got a phone call from her — she had just flown in from Paris and needed a place to crash and sleep, so I said, Yes, yes, come over. Her face was thinner than I had remembered and her faintly asymmetrical sea-green eyes darker. She had come back because she was two months pregnant and had begun to have cramps, and the next morning in my apartment when she woke up she was bleeding. I got her to the emergency room and stayed until the nurse's aide took her away in a wheelchair, then the next day I went back and watched her while she slept. I felt oddly hollow, as if some place inside me was empty.

We talked the next day, a little, and she went home to Newburyport. A couple of months later I sent her an invitation to a Boston show I was in, but she didn't reply and I figured she had gone back to Paris. I moved to New York, began to paint like an abstract expressionist and tried to mingle with the big names at the Cedar Tavern, but I got a horrible case of influenza and when I recovered I saw that my New York paintings were crap. I set fire to every canvas in my studio and was tossing the flaming shit out the window when somebody said, "Hey, Renato!" and she wasn't in Newburyport or Paris but here in my doorway. "I thought you were going to Paris!" I said.

"I'm leaving tomorrow. What are you doing?"

"I'm getting rid of some rotten paintings."

"I was on the sidewalk hunting for your address when these pieces of fire began to fall out of the sky. I thought it might be you." So we had a breakfast together and she said she'd write to me and, as I didn't write good letters, I said I'd send her sketches.

We corresponded and although she was still completing her work at the Sorbonne, she found a group of painters and writers and moved in with a forty-year-old man from England — a "savage intellectual who holds all social conventions in contempt," to precisely quote her letter.

I was astonished by how injured I felt, and angry at myself for feeling that way, and confused because I couldn't square anything in my mind — after all, I had gone to bed with Sophia and later with Odine and still later with Bena, and I'd never expected Alba to live like a nun. I couldn't go to Paris so I went to Montreal, to the French side, and visited an old papermaker I had known at the Museum School, and through him I met a young crowd of artists and Québécois Separatists, including Denise, a lively young woman who that first evening started to undress in my room. I said, "Wait!" and told her I was visiting Montreal only for a couple of weeks, at which she hesitated and then smiled, saying, "C'est bon cela," and pulled her jersey off over her head.

I spent the winter on Cape Ann, working for my aunt Gina who had a café there, and the following spring my friend Costas and I hitchhiked up the coast with our painting gear, aiming for Monhegan Island and those scenes where Robert Henri and his friends had done some great paintings. We never got to Monhegan, but we painted out-of-doors and though I didn't get much done, it was a lot better than painting in a hole in New York or thinking I was an abstract expressionist.

By midsummer I was back in Massachusetts, flat broke, so got a job repainting a 1930s WPA mural in a country restaurant, Lorette's Farm, a long, rambling structure where I worked at night when the place was empty and slept during the day in a stifling room in the restaurant's attic. One dawn while heading to bed I met young Nancy Lorette, who made pastry early in the morning, "Before the busybody spies are awake," she told me, laughing. One thing led to another, as philosophers say, meaning young Nancy and I met each morning on my way to bed. Then at ten each night her mother, Avril Lorette, would rap briskly on my door to wake me just when my room was getting cool enough to sleep in, and if I didn't promptly pull on my pants and go to the door she would come in and shake my shoulder, her hands scented with the blissfully cool odors of carrot greens, celery, fennel and apple. I'll make no excuses; one thing led to another with Mrs Avril Lorette, too.

When my various duties to the Lorettes were coming to an end, I decided to avoid bad scenes by leaving quietly, or you could say stealthily, so instead of going directly downstairs I ducked from my bedroom into the next attic, heading for the last attic and the ladder down to the storeroom. I was creeping along a rafter, dragging my easel and paint box, and was just about there when I set my knee on a rotted timber and plunged through the ceiling into the room below. I staggered around in a rain of crumbling plaster, splintered lath and two-hundred-year-old dust, and bumped into Alba. "Renato!" she cried.

"I thought you were in Paris!" I said.

"I got back a month ago and began working here last week. What are you doing?" she asked, brushing plaster bits from my shoulders.

"Murals. But right now I'm running away," I said, grappling with my easel and paint box.

The Lorettes' voices came from an upstairs room, shouting at each other.

"You're running away from Mrs Lorette?"

"Her, too."

"From Nancy Lorette? From both?"

"Not my fault. It's complicated," I said.

"You mean you —" Alba had begun to laugh. "With both of them? I *bet* it's complicated."

"Got to get going," I said, briskly.

She gave me a quick smile. "You can take Jack's car."

"Who's Jack?"

"He is," Alba said, nodding toward an athlete in a red-striped jersey who came marching through the doorway with a large, heavy sack on his shoulder — a guy she favored, I'm sure. "Give him the keys, Jack."

I got a place in Boston in a building that was scheduled to be demolished, so the rent was cheap, and if you looked between the other tenements you could see big slices of the Charles River and Cambridge on the other side. I was invited to exhibit in a group show in Cambridge. It was a good group and my work stood out as especially strong, so I invited Alba. She came and I remember clearly how she looked walking toward me — the trim jacket, the blazing white of her throat and the stiff rise of her breasts, the tight skirt — her hair in a thick glossy French twist, silver button earrings, a flashy bracelet and high heels. The show-room attracted a pleasingly full crowd and I met the other painters as well as the owner of a big gallery in Boston. I introduced Alba to my parents and my brother, Bart, then afterward we five went to a Greek restaurant to celebrate, and when dinner broke up, everybody hugged everybody and they drove off, leaving Alba and me on the sidewalk.

That night we walked from the restaurant to the Charles River and then along the Charles, and as the sun came up behind Boston — the old Boston, the gold dome of the State House on the hill and a blurred mosaic of bricks and brownstones making the low city — the light came in pale blue shafts between the buildings and onto the dark glassy river to where we were standing side by side, our elbows on the railing above the edge of the water, talking and talking. Our arms brushed and — Oh! — I turned and found her watching me, waiting. Her face was bare again, the way it had been years ago, and I could see all there was to see, one eye almost invisibly larger than the other, the dark sea-green irises flecked with uneven rays of lighter green and blue, the high contour of her cheek, the nakedness of her lips, and when I kissed her mouth I got light-headed and had to grab the rail to keep from plunging into the river.

We began to walk the long bridge across the Charles, but it got longer and longer, so when a cab came by we flagged it down and rode the rest of the way to my place. When I opened the door I saw how bad it looked, so stark, with nothing but a table, a bed, some chairs and my big canvases. "Oh, I like this,"

Alba said. I watched her as she walked around the room, looking at my paintings, then she turned and said, "I love being here. All the colors. And these are so much bigger than the ones at the exhibit. I —" But she broke off as I had put my hands inside the lapels of her jacket to wrench it open so hard the silver button leapt off and hit the floor, ringing like a bell, and I yanked the jacket down her arms and pulled it off, and by then we were whispering so swiftly not even our guardian angels could have caught what we said.

"Do you believe in God?" she asked afterward. We were naked on our hands and knees, looking under the bed for her missing button.

I told her I hadn't made up my mind about that.

She said, "I mean, is life just things bumping into other things and everything happening accidentally? Because if it is, then how did we meet and keep on meeting? If it's all just atoms banging into other atoms it doesn't make sense. But I feel it must make sense."

All I knew was I wanted her for the rest of my life.

"There must be a meaning — Ah!" she cried, holding up the button. She got to her feet and shook her head vigorously to untangle her hair, then began to pull a comb through it, which was a pleasure to watch as I remembered her raking her fingers through that mop to catch out the straw after we had lain in the field up back of her house. "I was only fifteen," she said, as if I had spoken.

"Fourteen, Ka-gi-gi, you were still fourteen."

❦

Tomorrow is Valentine's Day and I've sent flowers to the girls and, you know, there are days when I'd just as soon be dead as alive. I can't get used to the idea that I'm going to be lonely for the rest of my life. You were everyone else.

❦

Another letter arrived from Leo Conti, this one saying that by a stroke of good fortune he had been able to acquire "excellent gallery space on Newbury Street. And, Renato, I hope you notice that I said ON Newbury Street." He didn't include the address. He did say that he was having the interior redone — "stripped down to the brick walls and completely reconceived." He had been told that the space previously housed a shop that sold expensive grand pianos or expensive neckties, he couldn't recall which. He said my work was essential and he wanted to see it. "I insist, Renato, I insist." He would give me a call when he was on his way out here — with warm regards, Leo.

I didn't care piss about gallery space or Newbury Street, and I didn't know what to do with Leo's letter. I pushed it back into its envelope and set it on Alba's desk, then I got my auger, spiles and buckets, and went to tap the two sugar maples out front. We had lived here six months when the giant up the road happened by and told me, "I could loan you a couple of spiles and buckets." I asked what spiles were for. "To tap those sugar maples," he said. So that became something Alba and I did together every year when winter retreated. As the snow softened and began to sink away, we would be outside emptying the buckets into big pails, lugging those into the kitchen to boil down the sap, the kitchen windows fogging over with maple-scented steam. I still have some syrup, the last we made together, each jar neatly labeled in Alba's handwriting.

Here and now, after that job was done, I put away my auger and clomped over to the studio, but as soon as I stepped inside I knew I didn't want to be there, so I shut the place up again and clomped back to the house, wondering why I had tapped the maples when there was only me and no Alba, and why I was trudging back and forth across this stretch of snow and mud. I phoned Scott, but got no answer and left no message. I got in my car and drove to the Barista stand for a cup of coffee. I thought I'd ask Shannon what she did after her husband died and the year rolled on day by day and came again to the day when he had died, but she looked oddly sullen, so I asked her how the day was going. "I've had better," she said, pressing the lid onto the cup and handing it to me.

"What does that mean?"

"It means Fitz is full of patriarchal shit and wants to control my life. Him and his community college education."

"He seemed nice enough, the couple times I met him."

"He interviews well, if that's what you mean. — He thinks I'm going to change what I eat and give up cigarettes, all for him."

"Maybe he just wants you healthy."

"I told him, I got needs and right now I need to be left alone. So he goes off to sulk and drink too damn much, but he's feeling romantic and makes his move, and I tell him, Fuck off! and he shoves me so hard I hit the wall, so I tell him, You fuckin' touch me again and your kids'll be seeing you in Billerica on visitors' day!" She began to scrub the counter.

All I said was, "Oh," because Billerica is where the Middlesex County Jail is, and I didn't know what else to say.

"The next morning he apologizes and tells me he'll understand if I want him to pack up and get out — like I'm some kind of cold-hearted bitch." She tossed the washrag aside. "He's working three jobs," she added.

"Bad weekend," I said.

"What about yourself?" she asked. "Anything new?"

"No one's going to move in and ask me to change my menu, if that's what you mean."

She smiled. "You never can tell," she said.

"I can tell."

I went back to my car and drove home in the fading light, stopping at Big Valley Farms to buy a loaf of bread and some olives. The tall lights blazed white over the parking lot. As I got out of the car a young woman came by in a short coat and long dress or skirt — a flowing garment such as Alba would wear — and a child, a toddler, was riding tucked inside her arm, her own small hand clutching her mother's coat collar. The woman had long chestnut hair, almost like Alba's. I paced myself to follow them into the store, but inside, the young woman stopped to seat her kid in the grocery cart and I was obliged to pass them. I picked up a loaf of multigrain, and a mix of pitted Kalamata and green olives stuffed with pimientos. I turned into the next aisle and here was the young mother who just now had stopped her shopping and was leaning forward over the grocery cart to bring her face closer to her daughter's, the two of them smiling and radiant with happiness at having each other so close. She was saying something to her daughter, while the daughter put her finger across her mother's lips, as if to hush her. I hesitated, then started to edge sideways past them and the woman glanced up at me and smiled. I returned her smile and said, "Fortunate child to have such a mother," and she said, "Oh, she's wonderful."

When I pulled into the frozen mud driveway the house looked deserted for years, the windows empty and black and bare. I went in and walked from room to room, turning on the lights, pulling down the shades and closing the curtains. I sat on the sofa in a storm of tears and howled up at the ceiling to Alba, "Help me!"

☙

The anniversary of Alba's death was coming close and closer and I decided I wanted to see her medical records. My brother said, "Why do you want to do that?" and I told him I needed to know why she had died in agony. When I mentioned it to Fletcher, he didn't say anything for a moment and then asked, "Won't that upset you terribly? Why upset yourself?" I told him I was ready now. So stubborn old Renato brought proof of who he was to the clinic and the quiet-spoken woman in the records department gave him a cardboard folder three inches thick with Alba's medical papers. At home he took out the papers and saw they were stacked chronologically, the ones from the hospital on top, and some of those were handwritten. Stupid old Renato poked down a few pages from the top and began to read, but discovered he couldn't go on reading and began to cry. Now see old runny-nose Renato as he hurriedly gathers the papers in his shaky hands and stuffs them back in the folder and walks from room to room in his deserted house, embracing the folder of papers hard against his chest, all the while sobbing and saying, "Don't worry, Alba, I'll take care of you, I'll take care of you, I can do it, Alba, don't worry."

☙

I tapped the maples, though I don't know why — a

plate of ice in the bucket some mornings and the wind with a razor edge. Let the bucket hang there too long and it's so full it spills when you lift it; take it off when it's less and you have to go out twice as often. Boiling down means forty quarts of sap gets us one quart of syrup. Take it off the stove too soon and it's watery; leave it on too long and it's scorched. I did it the way we always did, but there was zero pleasure doing it without you.

❦

On the first day of spring, Astrid phoned and so did Brizio, and Skye drove here for lunch, because Alba died one year ago on this day. I took Skye to an Indonesian restaurant and we talked mostly about the year she and Eric and the kids had spent among the Dayaks. Skye drove home, having chosen a pair of her mother's silver earrings shaped like small scallop shells and a jar of our maple syrup. Afterward, the house was empty and I walked around, not knowing what to do. The kids had been coming and going about once a month, but I still felt desolate when anyone left. Zoe and Emerson had purposely invited me to dinner this evening so I knew I was going there, and that was good to look forward to. I pulled on my parka and walked the streets where we had walked so often. When I got home I sat at the kitchen table and cried for a while, thinking of Alba and how terribly God had treated her.

I didn't know what to do. I made a cup of coffee and was still at the kitchen table when the phone rang. It was Leo Conti, telling me he was coming out to look at my work and was already on the road. Conti must have called as soon as he crossed the town line because only ten minutes later he swung his beige Mercedes into my rutted driveway, producing a big muddy splash. He got out of the car, gazed around and beamed. "Here I am again, a city boy in the country. I love it out here. Healthy air. Healthy trees. Very healthy trees. — How do I look?" He was upholstered in a thick red-and-black plaid shirt, a pair of heavy L.L.Bean boots, and a red-and-black plaid cap with fleece earflaps.

"You look ready for a winter in the Maine woods," I said.

"Exactly. I'm prepared."

"But this is Massachusetts in spring."

"You can't be too careful," he said. "Now let's go to the garage and see those works you've been keeping sequestered out here."

"Out here we call these structures barns." We headed that way.

"I thought barns were bigger and painted red," he said.

"When we got through building this, it cost as much as the house."

We went inside, the air dim and quiet and colder than outside. We climbed the stairway and as soon as we entered the studio, Conti said, "Ah, wonderful! I like it up here. And the view, the view. Fantastic!"

I reminded him that I hadn't done the view, but

by then he was already looking at some old canvases. "You can move them around, do whatever you want," I told him. "And there's three in that crate I was going to send to Worcester, if you want to look at them." I turned on the heat. Then I began clearing the work-table, just to have something to do while he focused on the paintings. Leo didn't say anything. For the next several minutes, he shuffled the stretchers, set this one or that one up against the wall, then simply stood there, absorbing it, his gaze flicking this way and that over each canvas, as if he were alone in the room.

"Great!" he said, startling me. "This is all good stuff, excellent, fine. But what I'm here for are the frescos you told me about years ago."

"I junked the frescos. It would take me a lifetime to get fresco colors the way I want them. I haven't got that long."

Leo ignored what I had just told him. "I want to look at them," he insisted.

They were downstairs, so we went downstairs. I opened half the shutters to let in some light, then pulled the sheets away and we looked at them. I should have destroyed them years ago. I didn't care a piss what anybody thought, I still didn't like the way the into-naco had soaked up the colors.

"Ah," he said. "Good. Very good." I didn't think so, but Leo had a faint smile on his face, as if he'd forgotten it there, and a distant speculative look in his eyes. "Now show me the big canvases, the ones you said you were going to install in this barn. — Where they'll get ruined with mold, I might add."

I opened the rest of the shutters, letting the barn fill with light, and pulled the sheets from the paintings that stood against the walls.

"Ah, yes," Leo said. He stood there and didn't say a word for a few moments, and then he added, "This is why I have a gallery."

I was pleased and then surprised that I was pleased.

❦

After Alba died I felt like smashing everything to bits — the frescos, the seccos, and all the canvases — everything I'd brought together for the big jigsaw mural. I had filled the scene with my entire extended family, my friends and acquaintances, had brought them together at a big dinner, some of which was in the house around the table while even more was outside on the grass or among the old apple trees, under an afternoon sun, for everyone was there, mostly clothed, some unclothed, the young, the old, the dead and those not yet born, everyone talking, gesturing, listening, eating, or, like my mother and Alba's grandmother Agnes and others, in the kitchen preparing the meal, my father uncorking the wine, and also outside playing horseshoes with Alba's father or bocce with my uncle Zitti and my friend Vanderzee, arguing about art or baseball or politics, while the little ones, the toddlers, ran here and there.

Maybe I got the idea from the corkboard we had on the kitchen wall. At first that was where we tacked the kids' school bus schedule and appointment cards for the dentist, things like that, but then we added snapshots, and over the years we kept some photos there permanently — little Astrid standing up in her crib, my beautiful mother at twenty-one, Alba's father in his greenhouse, age fifty — so, unlike the photos in an album, these lost all sense of chronology and existed companionably with each other. For the mural — for all the paintings, actually, but especially for the big mural — I painted, or tried to paint, in a way not slapdash, not hasty, but with the freedom you have when you're sketching, so that even the way the paint was applied would show pleasure, deep pleasure, and I altered perspective now and then, so it looked like the wine bottle might tip out of the frame or one of the toddlers fall into your arms. I had wanted to flood the scene with so much life it would obliterate death. That was just another of my vanities and reason enough to trash the whole damned thing now. But Alba had liked it. She said I was painting better than ever, that I was at the top of my form.

※

So that was the first year. Before Alba died I had thought the bereaved wept because they missed the person who had died and they felt so alone, and yes, I missed Alba so much I wanted to die, but I howled because of what had happened to her, because of her struggle in pain and terror, her agony as she knew she was dying. And she is only one, as I am only one, a drop in this ocean — one *stilla* in this *mare*, as Zitti used to say, making a play on my last name. This is happening to people every day, all over the world. Crying over myself came in the second year while standing in the shower, or alone at the dinner table, or climbing the weary steps to the bedroom at the end of the day.

I had tried to hold on to our life together. Every Sunday morning I dressed up, just as we used to do, and I set out the snowy Royal Worcester plates and those beautiful cups, white as water lilies, instead of thick mugs, and I made a good breakfast with cut-up fruit, orange juice, toast and honey, and all the things we used to have if it was just us two and no guests for brunch. Then I'd eat the breakfast and read the Sunday newspaper at the empty table in the silent kitchen. After a while, holding on felt worse than letting go. I don't know how many nights I lay in bed waiting for sleep, her ring in my fist on my chest.

I put off going to bed, fearing sleep, because I was afraid I'd dream about Alba and wake to find her gone and be devastated all over again. But I rarely dreamed and when I did we were in a crowd and she would drift ahead, farther and farther ahead, until she was lost to me, or, what was worse, she would simply leave for no reason, no dispute, no anger, nothing. She was never that way in life, never did anything between us without feeling, whether rage or desire, for which I'm grateful. During the day, memories would come of our life forty-five or fifty years ago, and those memories — images, but alive — of her bathing baby Skye or breastfeeding her. Or even further back, the drives we made all over New England, wherever I could find a teaching job or a gallery with wall space, the two of us shoulder to shoulder in that tiny VW Bug — no gas gauge, leaky sunroof — the memory so clear I could see her just as she was, this beautiful bright woman whose idea of a good time was to be in my company.

Somewhere back in this defective memoir I said I'd stop writing after I'd written about the first year. People let you grieve for a year, but after that you and your grief become an annoyance. For twelve months I had gotten through each day because I thought, without ever thinking about it, that life would get better, the way it always had after a disaster, but during the second year I saw it wasn't ever going to do that, because there was no better to get to — this was my life now and I hated it.

I had intended to stop, but here I am — scribble and scrawl — and I don't know why. I'm no closer to finding where Alba has gone and whether I can get to her without dying first, or if she no longer exists, as people say, though I still don't understand how she can be here one moment and cease to exist the next. Above all, I cannot see the point of this universal dying. When I write a note to Alba, it makes sense and I know what I'm doing, but I don't know why I continue to fill these sheets of paper.

As Denise said in her Christmas card, the second year is no better than the first. It's the same loneliness, the same abrupt collapse into tears, the same sobbing or howling, which no one wants to listen to and I don't want to talk about, and the only new thing is a growing ability to fake a life and behave like an ordinary person when other people are around. When I began this crappy chronicle, I said — or should have said if I didn't — that I'm writing this three, or now four, years after Alba died. I know she's gone and I know she's not coming back. But the other day I came into the house and saw Alba, who had finally found her way home, curled up asleep on the sofa, and even as I realized it was only our rumpled bed quilt, I knew she'd explain what had happened and how she had struggled to come home sooner, and why we had been left behind to believe she had died.

I may have written some of these events in the wrong order, scribbling things as they came to mind, and I won't bother to straighten them out because I want to finish this neuralgic scrawl before I die. We had a snow shower in late March or early April, the big flakes tumbling gently through the air and melting as they settled on the black street. The lawns along the street were white, with blades of green grass showing through here and there. I drove home through the peaceful snowfall, turning down this street and that

one to go past our familiar places, all the while thinking of Alba, pretending she was sitting beside me. That
may have been three years ago or last year.

❧

By the way, I did get around to reading that Lucretius book, *On the Nature of Things*, as my uncle Zitti
had recommended. There it was, this small, thick, red
book (ragged lines of Latin poetry on the left page,
dense blocks of English on the right), and me, making my clumsy trek across it, like stumbling over every
furrow of a plowed field. It turned out to be a book of
atomic physics by a well-off Roman who hobnobbed
with Cicero and Catullus. After the first dull pages
it began to get interesting, mostly because the author
was curious about every detail of the material world —
the only kind of world there is, he says — and he had
a theory that explained all of it. The book dazzled me.

According to Lucretius, in the beginning there's
only this great void through which atoms fall endlessly, the heavier and the lighter falling at the same
speed, no one atom overriding another; but now and
again a spontaneous swerve occurs, two atoms con-
nect, and one connection leads to another and another
and so on to the creation of things, little things that
add up endlessly and eventually lead to world upon
world —infinite worlds in infinite space. That swerve
was important to Lucretius, not only because it starts
the compounding of matter, but also because it has no

cause. It just randomly happens. So there is no iron chain of cause and effect to create a predetermined universe in which everything that happens was set at the beginning; absolutely not, the atoms simply swerve, and from those gratuitous swerves eventually comes our free will, he says.

Lucretius is more than a physicist; he's a moral philosopher who wants us to know we're free from such things as fate or destiny. And he announces early on that he's writing this book about the nature of things to liberate us readers from fear of the gods, fear of death and the afterlife, for as people are shown that the gods have no part in the creation or management of things, and once they see that all creation, including their own living body, is composed of atoms and nothing more, they'll understand that there is no life after death, no afterlife in which to suffer and fear. You, your body and your soul, are that collection of atoms and when they disperse there's no you — it's as simple as that. Lucretius's own personal atoms, body and soul, had dispersed two thousand and more years ago, and four or five hundred years later Saint Augustine died, his body but never his soul, which leaves me hanging, because I would have enjoyed introducing those two know-it-alls to each other.

"They'd make lousy dinner guests," Zocco says. "They'd end up in a food fight."

I hadn't seen Zocco for months, so I phoned him and we got together at a restaurant in Cambridge.

"No food fight," I said. "We'd have dinner here. Just the four of us — me, you, Augustine and Lucretius. They'd respect us because of our age. We're older than Augustine was when he died, and twice as old as Lucretius. Age has its prerogatives."

"I'd rather have sex."

"No, we're going to have food," I told him.

Zocco shrugged and opened his menu. "I can do that. I'm still pretty good at food."

There was a time when Lou Zocco and Cormac McCormac and Marvin Kadish and Tom Hay and I would meet — sometimes by chance, sometimes by plan — at the Café Paradiso. But the Paradiso was long gone and so was McCormac, and Kadish, too, and Tom Hay wasn't doing so well, either. Now Zocco and I had found this restaurant on Brattle Street that looked all right, especially as the windows were scrimmed with fog so the traffic outside was just blurred reds, yellows, and blues.

I don't recall what Zocco ate, but I had Italian onion soup flavorful enough to almost distract me. I asked about his wife, who had broken a bone in her foot. She was doing well, but old bones take a long time to heal, he said, much longer than you'd expect. He asked how I was doing and we talked about doctors for a brief while and about the stent that had been implanted in one of his coronary arteries a few years back. We complained about being busy and agreed that having too much to do was better than hanging around wih nothing at hand. "I don't know what people who have real jobs do when they retire," Zocco said. I told him they move to Florida and play golf. "I'd go crazy," he said. "What's keeping you busy these days?"

"I shop for food, I cook, I eat, I clean up afterward. I fix leaky faucets. And every so often I think about painting and that's exhausting."

Zocco laughed. "Have you noticed how everything is so much harder and takes longer to do? When I look at some of the crazy jobs I did. Or tried to do. Remember those big plywood prints I made? I couldn't do that today."

"Those were great," I said. Zocco had made prints from huge sheets of plywood by cutting away parts of the top layer and brushing inks or paints on what remained, then covering the block with a sheet of paper big as a tablecloth and pressing it with another sheet of plywood. "I liked them."

"I made all that paper. And I had to use a paint roller to spread the inks around." He smiled, remembering. "If I got one good print out of four tries, I was lucky."

We talked about papermaking and that led to his asking had I seen Sebastian Gabriel and Avalon recently and what were they up to, so we talked about them, and later about Winthrop who I hadn't seen since he moved to Plymouth to be near his son. I said, "I think it's all those toxic lacquers and acrylics he used that rotted his nerves. His wiring was pretty far gone the last time I saw him."

"Now it's like he blew a fuse in his brain," Zocco said. "Sometimes he makes sense, mostly not so much. He's in hospice. He's dying."

"I'm sorry —" I had thought I was going to say something more, but nothing came to mind. I looked out the window at the passing colors and that was better.

Zocco sighed. "This is glum," he said.

"I'm going to order some caffeine, an espresso, a cappuccino, anything. That might help."

"Good idea," he said. So we drank coffee and talked about Augustine's soul and Lucretius's atoms, politics and bankers and money. It was good to see Zocco again.

Alba, you'll wonder what happened. They knocked down the old Franklin house in one day. They're going to build those condominiums, just like they planned to all along. They removed all the windows but didn't save any of the fancy curlicue wood trim, then big backhoes pushed in the sides until the house collapsed in a heap — broken studs, boards, shingles. Terribly cruel and sad to see. Then they scooped the broken heap up into trucks and hauled it away. Today big earthmovers were going back and forth over what used to be the Four Seasons Gardens, scraping it flat and smooth. I'm afraid when you see it again you'll think you're lost and not find your way home.

❦

Last year was mostly grayscale with no flavors and no smells, which I realized only later. Now, last autumn's apples are sunk brown and rotted in the long grass and Alba's gardens, those big flowerbeds she had made everywhere, are a flattened tangle of soaked, decaying leaves with reddish briars and hollow stalks sticking out every which way. After she died, the flowers must have come up by themselves to float their colors in the midsummer heat, but I hadn't seen any of it. Now all those roots and tubers were restless again, the whole amoral smelly rotten fecund world that didn't care shit about death or dying.

❦

"I'm getting good at arranging funerals," Shannon tells me. Her grandfather has died.

"I know it's a terrible time, but it sounds like you made it go well."

"First my mother, then Robert, and now my grandfather." She pressed the lid on the coffee cup and set it on the counter.

It was a sunny day and the light striking the countertop illuminated her face, a pretty woman, despite everything. I asked her what she thought about all this dying.

"I try not to think in that direction. What good did thinking ever do? There's no understanding it."

"I think about it all the time."

"Let me know if it gets you anywhere. — Did you want spice cake?"

I said yes. Shannon always slipped two slices into the bag instead of one. This time I studied her hands and saw only one piece go into the bag, but when I picked it up I felt the bulk of two.

"You're crazy. They're keeping track of every damn crumb," I told her.

"Fitz keeps track of what he delivers and what gets spoiled in transit, and I keep track of what I get and what gets tossed because it's stale or spoiled. The numbers balance, that's all that matters. — How are you doing these days?"

§

The ophthalmologist tells me that the intraocular pressure in my right eye is so high it's damaging my optic nerve and will eventually destroy my vision. We've had this conversation before, because the same thing happened in my left eye a few years ago. I've gotten acquainted with the anatomy of my eyes, my cloudy vitreous fluid and the clogged exit canals through which it flows. We tried eye drops and laser to lower the pressure, but nothing worked. Now he suggests surgery, the same as he did on the left eye, cutting into the network of canals to open a kind of casement widow to allow the fluid a way out. I don't plan to paint anymore, but as long as I'm alive I don't want to go blind. Andrews, the ophthalmologist, is a handsome, quick, athletic man, fifty-something years old, who listens impatiently whenever I ask a question or venture an opinion. I ask how often he does such surgery. "Every Monday," he says briskly. I tell him I'll think about it. They don't respect you if you say yes on the first go-around.

🦋

Alba, I was walking past where the Four Seasons Gardens used to be, where they're building those condos. They have batter boards lined up for foundations and a redwing blackbird flew around and landed on one of the stakes. The same kind of bird that used to nest there by the creek.

🦋

I received a letter from Elizabeth Prescott, whom I had never heard of, saying that she was writing an article on Cormac McCormac, and that she had been given my name by his wife, Karen, who spoke of me as a longtime friend of her husband. Ms Prescott hoped I would be willing to be interviewed about McCormac, the man and his work, and she would be happy to visit me for the interview at my home, my studio, or any place I preferred. She closed by saying she looked forward to my reply.

Cormac died maybe half a dozen years ago, whittled away by diabetes. He had been a big guy, built for carving ordinary New England stones into faces or parts of faces — an eye, an ear — then piling them up into cairns in his hayfield, and later in life he worked with big pieces of metal, happy with his anvil and his acetylene torch. Karen was his fourth wife. I never met his first wife, but I recall his second as a young woman with lightly flushed cheeks, as if simmering with passion or, as it turned out, resentment, while his third made a career of meeting famous artists in their beds, and the fourth was Karen, who turned out to be just right. I knew Karen had been struggling to place his sculptures in museums and private collections, but since Cormac had died the only thing written about him was a five-inch obituary in the *Boston Globe*.

Elizabeth Prescott and I agreed to meet for the interview at a restaurant in Lexington. For no particular reason I had expected somebody in her middle years but she looked to be about eighty, you could say elegantly thin or you could say bony, and with thick, silver-white hair. So she was old and I knew that I looked as old to her as she looked to me. She was pleasant, easy to talk with, and when lunch arrived she turned on her recorder and we began to discuss Cormac, with her occasional questions — a quiet, unemphatic voice — to lead the conversation. So we talked through lunch, the waitress cleared the table, brought our coffee, and Prescott asked had Cormac ever spoken about a personal artistic vision, a philosophy or esthetic that he hoped to embody in his work. I think I laughed. I said no, and told her that what struck me most about Cormac and his work was how he loved the physicality of it. He loved muscular work, loved lifting boulders or hammering metal, and he loved that his creations took up residence in three dimensions, so you could walk around them and touch them. I answered a few more questions about Cormac, then Prescott turned off her recorder.

"Thank you so much," she said, relaxing and letting her shoulders, which had been stiff as a coat hanger, droop ever so slightly. "Karen speaks very highly of you."

"Karen's very kind. I should try to get over to their place one of these days. It's somewhat out of the way. — What are you writing, exactly?"

"Karen and I met in college and we've kept in touch through the years. And since Cormac died she's been trying so hard, desperately and without much success, to establish, or reestablish —"

"I know. I've seen other widows try that. It's heartbreaking work."

"I'm not really a writer. I majored in art history in college and I've taught art history and written a few academic articles, and in Karen's eyes that makes me a writer who —. Well, anyway, she's asked me more than once if I could write a piece about Cormac and, well, I thought I'd try to help. — And my own husband died four years ago," she added.

"Oh, I'm so sorry," I said.

She hesitated. "I learned from Karen that your wife —." She broke off.

"Yes."

"I'm sorry," she said.

"You were happily married," I said.

"Yes, very."

"I think of Alba every day. She's always there. Or here."

She smiled. "I used to think that was just a nice way of saying you missed your husband or wife, a polite way to talk about grief. But it's so true. You think of a person every day, sometimes it feels like all day. We did everything together."

"Do you have children?"

"Yes, thank God. And three grandchildren."

I asked about her husband and their life together. He had been a lawyer ("wills and mortgages and so forth") but he also did trial work for liberal causes ("obscenity cases, religious cases and things like that"). "We never got rich, but we were never poor. It was a good life." She smiled just a bit, then looked away and let her mind drift. "We liked being together," she said. "We enjoyed each other."

All the while she talked I imagined how she would have looked decades ago, her cheeks higher, full and firm, her jawline sweeping to the smooth column of her neck, for now the sacks beneath her eyes were flat and discolored and the cords along her throat hung as slack as my own. She had been loved and made love to for years, a loving and desirable woman.

"He died of emphysema. Which was horrible and unfair," she said, her voice rising in anger. "He never smoked. A little marijuana in the early years, but that's all. When we were young he ran marathons. And in the end we had to carry bottles of oxygen with us wherever we went." She sighed, looked at me again, smiled.

I said, "Cormac once told me he didn't understand death. He asked me, What's it for? What's the point?"

We talked a while longer and I thought how decayed I must appear to Elizabeth Prescott, as she does to me, and how the both of us must look to others, a very old pair sitting at a restaurant table, chatting over their coffee long after the waitress has brought the check. I said, "This conversation has been a pleasure," and she said, "The pleasure was mine," and I said, "Maybe we can get together again," and she said, "I'll be in touch to show you what I've written."

❦

Yesterday I bought a big copper weather vane to mount on the barn — an angel flying and blowing a long trumpet, the same angel as the little ornament we set at the top of the Christmas tree. No one will think I'm crazy because I put up a weather vane, and you'll see it from far off and you'll know you're coming to the right place. If I have to move to that desolate college town where Skye lives, I'll take the weather vane along and also paint the front door same color as here, so you'll still be able to find me.

🙖

As they grew older, my uncles Nicolo and Zitti began to change their views on politics and God and everything else they always talked about, as if after all those years of disputing with each other, each had finally convinced the other of his rightness. Premises and logical deductions had clearly proven weak and unreliable for both of them. "I don't know," uncle Nicolo would say. "In fact, the older I get, the less I know." At which uncle Zitti, agreeing, would smile ever so slightly and say, "Well, in a few years we'll be dead and it won't matter what we know or don't know."

"Zitti, please!" Candida told him. "We're beginning a new year. Don't be depressing."

That would have been New Year's Day in 1976 at my parents' home. Everyone's eyesight had faded to the point where they each had a shade of night blindness and didn't drive after dark, so instead of having a New Year's Eve party my mom had invited them to celebrate New Year's Day in the early afternoon with tea or coffee, which you could have decaffeinated if you wished, and with sweetener instead of sugar, if you wanted, plus true biscotti and tiramisu.

"We'll be pushing up daises," Marissa said, sounding cheerful.

"Who wants more tea or coffee?" my mother asked,

hoping to change the topic. "Renato, ask Alba if she wants to come in to get warm."

I told her Alba was fine in her warm parka and wanted to keep an eye on the kids. I didn't add that she was happy to have escaped outside with our children and my old Flexible Flyer sled which she'd taken from the cellar. I watched my father dip the end of his biscotto into his coffee and lift it with a deft roll of his fingers to shake off the lingering drop. "Is it that time moves faster as we get older," he said, "or is it just that we move slower?"

They looked unchanged to me, even though I knew it wasn't so. After all, my mother's hair was not the tumbling blue-black river of ink it had been when I was a kid, but gray, gray as Marissa's and Candida's hair. Last summer at an outdoor wedding reception, Uncle Zitti had slumped in his garden chair, his left arm having abruptly quit working, which sent him to the hospital for three days. "A very minor stroke, completely recovered now," he said, and he refused to speak about it ever again. Uncle Nicolo had slowed down and he didn't walk quite properly but shuffled and listed to one side like a wounded ship. My father had arthritis and elevated blood pressure and he complained of forgetfulness, but he looked fine and vigorous. Two winters ago he had finally ceased cutting stone and had put his tools away for the last time, and that summer he and my mom drove up to Montreal, and this past summer they stayed at the Château Frontenac in Quebec.

The conversation had drifted to political gossip — uncle Nicolo saying it looked like the Cold War was ending, Zitti declaring a different war would certainly start up someplace, my father insisting you could never trust the Soviets, Marissa and Candida saying the whole world was tired of war — and from there the talk turned to the grandchildren and then to what they were being taught in grammar school these days. Nicolo said that when he was a kid the president of Harvard announced you could get a liberal education by reading fifteen minutes a day from his five-foot shelf of books, the Harvard Classics. "There were three things I wanted to have — the Harvard Classics, the *Encyclopædia Britannica*, and a grand piano. Now we have all three." He laughed just a bit and it was impossible to say whether he was making a modest boast or tossing off a jest.

"Your son knows that story," Marissa reminded him. "And he admires you. He's told you so."

Nicolo nodded in agreement. "Yes, he did." He lingered over the thought.

I asked him what was his favorite book from the Harvard Classics.

He brightened. "Darwin. *On the Origin of Species*. It made a deep impression on me. I was fascinated by his theory of evolution. — I was so dazzled I didn't notice the dark side of it," he added.

"You see," Zitti said, turning to me. "He's changed his mind about science."

"No. I still think it's a beautiful theory, and a right one," Nicolo said. "But I've come to see evolution as tragic and wasteful. I understand how people were upset by Darwin because he said that we evolved from earlier creatures — from monkeys, as they used to say. But what's most disheartening to me is that all life arises from accidents and not because of any plan or purpose in nature. If every living thing is the result of randomness or chance or accident — call it what you want — the staggering, wasteful deaths, well —" He broke off.

"We can call it God, if you want," Zitti said. "That's the way God works his creation. Tragic and wasteful." He had finished his tiramisu and now wiped his lips with a napkin, sat back in his chair. "People have been going to church, pleading with God to behave more humanely, but so far with no luck."

"Zitti, please," Candida said. "No more about God."

Zitti laughed and opened his arms to dramatize his surprise and innocence. "I didn't bring God into this, Nicolo did," he said. "As far as I'm concerned, God is a waste of time."

"A little more coffee?" my mother suggested to everyone. "To warm up your cup."

"The longer I think about life, the more mysterious it gets," Nicolo said. "We began in some protoplasmic slime or green algae and here we are now, sitting around this table discussing our own evolution. It's stunning. I haven't thought this through but, despite the chanciness and accidents and despite all the randomness, there appears to be such a purposeful drive that . . . I don't know what to think."

My father told my mother, Yes, he'd like a little more coffee to warm his cup.

"I prefer not knowing what to think," Zitti announced. "I've always been a rationalist and a skeptic—"

I laughed. "You?" I said, interrupting him. "When did you become a rationalist and a skeptic? You must be joking."

"No. Remember, I've always liked Montaigne, a wonderfully curious and skeptical man. The older I get, the more I appreciate his refusal of certainty." He smiled. "He's an Italian, you know, transplanted to France." Zitti regarded French intellectuals as foppish dilettantes, and for those French thinkers or artists he did admire, he claimed they had Italian backgrounds.

"Can't we talk about something real for a change?" Candida said.

❦

What am I supposed to do now? I'm a painter who had eye surgery a few weeks ago, because otherwise I'll go blind faster, my left ear doesn't hear things clearly, all my joints ache, and if I sleep the wrong way I get a pain in my hip that feels like somebody hammered a spike in there. Alba, I still wake up in the morning hard — not *hard* hard, not like when we were younger, but hard enough. So what am I supposed to do now? You're the only woman I know who understands these things. This unruly thing especially. Your man from the sea.

❦

Katia Robinson drove up from Hartford to have lunch with me — little Katia Tsarevski, grown-up but not grown old, still very trim, still with that interested direct gaze. The Tsarevskis lived in the flat across the hall from the rent-free storage room I was using as a studio back then. Every so often I'd hear her parents' curses and rages, and skinny little Katia would come over to show me the artwork she had done in school that day. A few years later, when her mother and father got to worse fighting (screams, whacks, heavy thumps), she'd walk in with her schoolbooks and sit on the floor against the wall — knees up, underpants showing, a Balthus in my studio — and quietly do her homework while I stretched canvas or painted. Now she's about to become a grandmother. "In two weeks or so," she said.

"Raising children is the only worthwhile activity there is," I said.

She smiled. "You exaggerate, of course."

"Of course, but only a little."

"What have you been painting?" she asked.

"I haven't been painting."

We talked about my not painting and about her

leaving the nondenominational church where she had been ministering for a dozen years, and about her son and daughter-in-law, and I told her this and that about my children and grandchildren. Near the end, over coffee, we talked about Alba. "For me, she was like a heroine in a book," Katia said. "I mean, really beautiful."

"Yes, she was. And she stayed that way."

I drifted into silence, then Katia added, "Not only good-looking, but . . . one day I walked in and she was in your studio arranging flowers in a glass jar. She asked me to help her, and when we were finished she broke off a blossom and tucked it in my hair. I can't tell you how extraordinary that made me feel. I know you won't understand, but it made me feel beautiful and grown-up."

"That's the way she was," I said. "That was Alba."

"I wanted to be her. I was quite envious. Or jealous." Then Katia smiled and said, "I was a jealous girl."

"Jealous? No."

"Oh, yes. I'd hear you two going into your studio and I knew what you would be doing in there. You know, on that old mattress with the sheepskin furs."

"Oh God, no!"

"You've probably forgotten, but there was a day when I took off my blouse and was bare-chested. My idea of seduction."

I had been making silkscreen prints that day and was deep into the work, pulling and lifting, when she said, What do you think of this? So I turned around and saw her.

I laughed. "I haven't forgotten. But you were just a kid, that's all."

"You were stunned. Then you said, firmly, Put on your shirt and we'll go out and I'll buy you a maple walnut ice-cream cone. — You knew maple walnut was my favorite flavor that summer."

It was a good lunch. We parted with a hug and I drove home sick with desire for Alba who was gone, gone, gone.

⚜

I have plenty of time to think about the things I did. I don't meditate on the past, but every now and then a scene comes to mind, floats to the surface all on its own, and mostly it's from the early years, the two of us cozy in our second-hand VW bug (manual choke, no gas gauge) driving all over, or Alba breast feeding Skye, playing with Astrid, or just Brizio and me in the shower. Other times, it comes back like a punch in the face — my having said something that made Alba cry, or maybe it was the ugly tone of my voice. That's Renato.

Certain sexual follies don't look so disastrous from this end of life. Yes, Zoe is the mother of Astrid and so is Alba, which you understand or you don't. At the time it felt like we had wrecked ourselves, but there was nothing to do about it so we just kept on living, no matter how painfully, and after a few years we were just going along with the same ups and downs as everyone else. All that was when we were young, but we could be vain or foolish at any age. When I was seventy and Alba not much younger, we put ourselves on opposite sides of the Charles River. Alba slept in Cambridge in our overpriced Bauhaus box, a concrete columbarium with big windows and all our earthly goods. I slept in Boston in the studio with all my paintings, enough for a dozen different shows, none of which had happened in the last twenty years. I had been erased from the big art biz. But I had learned how to paint and was making a final attack on the galleries. Alba took up cooking with a visiting French chef.

That's when Avalon crashed from San Francisco and knocked at my studio door — a skanky looking woman with jewelry stuck to her face, flat broke, having nothing but a backpack and a little son with Asian eyes like inkwells. I didn't know her. Her father, Brendan Flood, had been a friend of mine, but he had died when Avalon was a kid and her mother died the day she was born. Being me, I let her in and they stayed a year.

I regret being vain, oblivious, stupid and petty, regret my rants and complaints, regret talking logic when I should have shut up and listened, regret being that me. Fortunately, Alba and I craved each other's company and, above all else, craved each other.

It was beginning to snow in tiny flakes, but I had decided to drive to Meg O'Brian's Trifles, a small shop in Cambridge crammed mostly with handmade jewelry, but also with scarves, fancy blouses, fripperies and second-hand clothes, all in a space no bigger than my kitchen. We both knew Meg, and I used to come here to buy Alba a little surprise — a silver seashell or a necklace of sea-glass — and I missed doing that. I longed to do it again, so I came here to get something for my granddaughters, the older ones, Danae and Chiara. And maybe I should mention right here that Meg knew Lucy Dolan.

Now Meg smiled and said, "Renato, it's good to see you," and, after a moment's hesitation, she added, "I heard, I'm so sorry." I said, Thank you, you're kind to remember. We chatted while I looked around, deciding at last on two pair of pendent earrings, glass with sparkling flakes of reddish gold inside. I confess, another reason I'd come here was so I could bring up Lucy. While Meg was putting the earrings into tiny cushioned boxes, I told her I'd bumped into Lucy and she'd told me she was going to open a bakery.

"Yes," Meg said. "She wanted me to go with her to look at a place she found, but things got busy here and I couldn't. She's calling it Peasant Bread and Fancy Pastries. I know she'll do well."

"Where is it?"

"She told me. But all I remember is it's in one of those towns out past Concord — Billerica, Acton, Westford — out that way."

❦

So the next day I drove alphabetically through snowbound towns northwest of Concord — Acton, Billerica, Boxborough, Carlisle, Chelmsford — until I found Peasant Bread & Fancy Pastries. It was a small shop, with a freshly painted yellow door and a display window where an athletic workman was coiling electric cable. I pulled open the door and a bell jingled overhead. Lucy Dolan, sliding a tray of cookies into the display case, looked up, saw me and smiled. "Renato! What a lovely surprise." Her wild thick hair was kept in check by a baseball cap with the word *Monterey* on the front.

"I was just driving through, so I thought I'd stop to say hello. — What a lie! I came hunting for your shop."

"And I'm so glad you found it."

The workman, who had hopped down from the window, smiled, told Lucy, "You're all set and good to go," and headed out to his rusty van.

"Tell me what you think," Lucy said. "Do you like it?"

I looked around. It was a bare square room with pale yellow walls, a big glass case with shelves of cookies and pastries, another case with loaves of bread, a marble-topped counter in between. "I like it very much."

"It's good, isn't it? There isn't much room out front here, but I was wondering if, anyway, I should have a couple of chairs and a small table. Make it more friendly and accommodating. And I need something for the walls."

"I like it," I told her. "It smells good in here."

She had a big beautiful smile. "Come around this way," she said. "I'll show you the bakery part."

The back room was brightly lighted and shining, divided by a long table with a gleaming stove on one side and, on the other side, some tall aluminum racks with wheels.

"It looks wonderful," I said.

"It's a lot of work and I'm exhausted," she told me. "But I love it."

She did look tired. She was only a few years older than my oldest daughter, but she looked older than that.

"I'm in love with my bakery shop," she continued. "Is that possible? Because it's my studio, like you have a studio to paint in and I have this to bake in."

"The nice thing about your art is that people pay you so they can take it home and eat it. It's great life-sustaining art."

"Renato, you're the only person in the world who sees my baking as great art."

I laughed. "But it is," I insisted.

"You're biased in my favor."

"That, too."

❦

You're right, there isn't enough counter space in the kitchen. And you're right about the roots from the maples making it near impossible to plant anything in the front flowerbed. I never knew how bothersome those things were. I'm trying to keep up the gardens and you know I'm not doing a good job. They were beautiful and I always said so, but I never knew how you did it and I still don't know.

❦

I liked talking with Shannon. This morning she was wearing more makeup than usual, maybe a bit too much. "You're looking good," I told her.

She pressed the lid on the coffee cup and handed it to me, saying, "Sure. And that's all that matters. Right?"

She looked angry and I didn't know what to make of that, so I didn't say anything. I took a sip of coffee.

"You can put lipstick on a pig and rouge on a corpse. Right?" she said, insistently.

I asked her what she was so sore about.

"Sore? I found a lump and the doctor says he wants me to wait and see. In my breast. I don't want to fucking wait and see. I want it out."

It felt like somebody had kicked my head. I asked did she like her doctor.

"Why should I like my doctor?"

"I mean, do you trust his judgment. Do you think he's a good doctor?"

"How would I know?"

I couldn't figure what to say next. I asked, "What does Fitz think about this?"

She didn't say anything for a moment, then she said, "Fitz is good. He's good. He understands my feelings about this fucking shit. I think he really does."

"You're going to be OK, Shannon."

"They cut Fitz's hours. The company is trying to look super-efficient because they want Starbucks to buy them or something. So they cut his hours and I have a lump. Everything rotten happens at once."

"They'll take out the lump if they need to. You're going to be you, no matter what."

"They scheduled me a biopsy tomorrow."

"Good. You're going to be all right."

"This is all I need."

I kept telling her she was going to be all right.

❧

Alba, I wish you could see this. Summer is here and the young women shopping at Big Valley Farms are dressed for a day at the beach. Those shorts that were shaped like boxes and went halfway to the knee — they're cut high this summer, beautifully high and tight, just like you said. The younger ones are close to naked and happy about it, just a half-jersey top and shorts, and the colors for toenails in this town are rose or tangerine. I know you'd come back if you could. At dinner tonight I pushed my dish aside and put my head on the table and cried.

᥿

The year wore on and I still didn't know where Alba had gone, and some days it was as if she had not been here at all, but she had been here and we had loved each other and I wanted to find her. Lucretius, writing his poem two thousand years ago, says that because space is infinite and the number of atoms is also infinite, you have to conclude that other worlds are being created out there, worlds populated by other people who, like us, are born and perish. Nowadays, up-to-the-minute physicists sound much like ancient Lucretius, for they have theories about other worlds and, in fact, whole universes, one beyond another without end. Lucretius builds his theory with step-by-step appeals to reason. I'm not wonderfully impressed by reason, though to say so is like farting in church. I mean, we have only a few ways of figuring things out and those ways are limited and fallible and it's a marvel we've come as far as we have with reasoning. Of course, these physicists who arrive at the same conclusion as Lucretius use complex mathematics to get there, but mathematics is an artifact composed by reason and when carried far enough it leads to logical paradoxes and madness.

Whatever I have of physics and mathematics comes from my uncle Nicolo. Uncle Nicolo used to present physics and mathematics as puzzles, and rather than boring me with the summation of an infinite series, he gave me Zeno's paradox of Achilles and the tortoise, and instead of quanta or wave equations, he treated me to the perplexing behavior of light. Light, he told me, passes through a solitary slit as a stream of chaotic particles, but through twin slits as a smooth continuous wave. As it happened, light had always intrigued me and by the time I enrolled at the Museum School it wasn't simply light but color that was my heart's desire.

Uncle Zitti told uncle Nicolo that he, Zitti, was gratified by the way light acted. It appeared incomprehensible to us mortals, Zitti said, because light was a singular manifestation of God, so close to God as to be synonymous with Him, which philosophers had recognized at least as far back as the ancient Greeks. "And that new structure they've just completed at MIT," he said, tapping a cigarette on his silver cigarette case for emphasis, "that chapel or meditation building or whatever they're going to call it — it has a square block of marble as an altar and a carefully designed hole in the roof, an oculus, so that light can descend right onto it. Even at Tech they sense that light is a divine, sacred essence." At which point Nicolo would smile, sit back, and polish his Ben Franklin spectacles.

Thanks to uncle Nicolo, I was enchanted not only by Newton's vanishing infinitesimals, but by the elegant mathematical design of his cosmos, the calculated swing of the moon around the earth, the gigantic sweep of the planets around the sun, the endless trajectory of a hyperbolic comet, all traveling the conic sections of Apollonius and all drawn through their celestial courses by gravity — "Which varies inversely with the square of the distance," uncle Nicolo would remind me. That Newtonian universe, where each part moved in time with all the others, appeared reasonable to me and, above all, beautiful.

Now as I was haunting this deserted house and not painting I had plenty of time to read and it was mostly physics I read, the mathematical physics that promised other worlds, quantum mechanics. I began with Werner Heisenberg, which led me into a quicksand of mathematics and, finally, to his matrices, those tic-tac-toe arrays of numbers which were meaningless to me, because I could feel no connection between them and the howling world I lived in. On the other hand, Erwin Schrödinger's wave equations were more approachable, sensuous and beautiful in their way. In fact, Schrödinger himself came through as more approachable and I was delighted to discover that he had called Heisenberg's mathematics repellent. Even the wave equations' Greek letter psi looked good to me — if you resonate to any of this, you're doomed — just as the sigmas had looked elegant sixty years earlier when I was taught calculus.

The infinitesimal world where light is a condensation of spectral photons isn't clear as day: it's a fog of probabilities. Schrödinger's wave equations can calculate those probabilities with exquisite precision — they give the right answers every time — but what those beautiful equations say about the nature of reality is open to interpretation. Of all the probabilities, only one comes to pass, but the equations don't say the other probabilities vanish; on the contrary, they are as real as they always were, continuing forward through time, not here, but in other worlds, real worlds beyond this one. That's what I was after. Schrödinger himself shies away from speculating on the meaning of the wave function, but I'd like to ask him directly.

"There's the problem of his being dead, of course," George said. That was George Agathos and we were moving my kitchen table out the back door and past the apple trees.

"I could write him a letter," I said. "Feynman wrote a letter to his wife a year and a half after she had died. It's a heartbreaking letter."

"And it ends with his saying he doesn't know where to send it. Richard Feynman had human longings. Some people would say he was all too human."

"Did you know him?"

"No, not really. I met him a few times at conferences. I listened to some of his talks. — You forgot to tell me why we moved this table."

We had carried it past the apple trees and had finally set it down in front of the barn.

"I'm going to strip off the lacquer, take it down to the wood and resurface it," I said. "I won't go deep. Just skim the surface." I didn't tell him I was worried that Alba wouldn't recognize it without the stains and gouges.

"I was hoping we were going to eat off it," George said. "I'm hungry."

"We *are* going to eat off it. I won't be working on it until tomorrow."

"Ah, we're dining alfresco! A picnic! Soon, I hope."

"As soon as we carry the food from the kitchen to the table."

"I'm ready."

George Agathos is the only person I know who is equally passionate about politics, quantum mechanics, and food. We brought chairs from the house and ate at the table in the cool of the barn doorway. I had made a pretty good salad — it had everything plus artichoke hearts and water chestnuts — along with a crusty Tuscan boule, some cheese and olives and a bottle of Soave.

"It's important to have wine," I said, filling his water glass with Soave. "So you'll know it's not breakfast."

George had shaded his eyes with his hand and was squinting past me. "There's a couple of small deer — fawns, I guess — over by the flower garden," he said.

I picked up a stone and threw it at them. They looked at us, then went back to nosing the grass.

"I think they know you," George said.

"They know I can't throw worth a damn. My arm is shot."

"It's a sunny day in June. Have some more wine. — Those were great brunches you and Alba had out here. Not here, exactly, but over by the house. The weather was always beautiful, too."

I don't know if you can really avoid thinking of something by trying not to, but I had tried to avoid that one. All I said was, Those were good times. Later he told me about the trip he and Io had taken to Europe and how they had visited the Large Hadron Collider. "It's a staggering piece of engineering," he said. "When that thing gets up to speed it will be seven times more powerful than any other collider anywhere." He talked about the smashup of subatomic particles at near the speed of light, the spray of exotic bits from the collision. He asked had I been doing any painting.

"No," I said. "But I miss it. I miss the desire to paint."

"It will come back."

"I don't know. Some things don't come back."

"What got you interested in Schrödinger?"

"His wave equations — how did he invent them and what do they mean?"

George smiled. "Oh, ho! You're thinking about him and that woman up in the Swiss mountains, snow outside, fire inside, making love and wave equations — fuck and scribble, fuck and scribble. That was the best two-week vacation in the history of physics."

"What do you think of the interpretation of the equations that says there must be other worlds?"

George squinted into the distance, as if to see the problem more clearly. "Ever hear the expression *Shut up and compute*?"

"Never."

"It means the equations give us the right answers — don't try to interpret them, just use them."

"You're not a big help, George."

He hesitated, then said, "I don't know if Alba is alive in another world, Ren. No one knows. Except maybe you," he added.

"Not me," I said. "I'm even less help to me than you are," I told him.

The air was warm and full of light. We drank the last of the wine, then took a slow walk up to the house with the dishes and leftovers, and back again for the chairs, talking of life on other worlds and theories of multiverses and, more locally, George's suggestion that I should lay out a bocce court on a nice stretch of flat grass alongside the apple trees. And so, goodbye. "That was a good lunch," George said. And, yes, it was a good lunch.

❦

Alba, I have to tell you they're carving out a big new shopping plaza on the next hill beyond Big Valley Farms. And it's amazing how rapidly they're building those condos where the Four Seasons Gardens used

to be. I pass it two or three times a day, and already I
can't remember exactly where the old Franklin house
stood. The places you and I used to walk are getting
erased — everything is getting erased and there'll be
no memory of us walking through that field, because
memories wither when you have them all by yourself.

☙

I hadn't seen Shannon for a month because she was
off having surgery to remove the lump from her breast.
"The lump was benign," she told me. "But the surgery
was a bitch and it hurt."

"Doctors lie," I said. "It's part of their routine. Surgery always hurts,"

"I liked the stuff they gave me in the hospital, but
when they sent me home all I had was Tylenol."

Shannon handed me my coffee and as nobody came
by we talked about surgeries and pain. I told her how
one of the surgeons working over me had messed up
and afterward I had to have a catheter for a couple of
months. "I had this hose shoved up me and a plastic
bag strapped to my leg, and at night I had a big bag
hanging from the bed and it would fill up with pee. In
the morning when I took a shower, Alba would sit on
the toilet seat and hold the bag while I showered."

"I did that for Robert when the brain cancer meant
he had no control anymore. He had a catheter like
that. I'd hold the bag and get in the shower with him."

"Oh."

"I didn't mind, but I was afraid he must feel humiliated or something —" She looked down at the scrub cloth and began to move it mechanically in a circle on the counter.

"He knew you loved him. You're the best thing that ever happened to him," I said. "You're the best."

That's what I think and I'm glad I told her. I saw her now and again, but a month or two later when I stopped at the stand a new woman was there who looked twenty-five and healthy. I asked if she knew Shannon. No, she didn't. I asked if she knew Fitz who delivers the supplies. She said, "The man who delivers supplies is named Fernando." I asked if the company had been bought by Starbucks. She looked blank for a moment, then said, "Do you want a coffee or a latte or something?"

❦

Leo Conti drove us to the Fête Champêtre, the expensive restaurant pretending to be a French farmhouse. Leo didn't have a wig today. His bald head was tanned and he wore a green translucent visor, rather like the ones worn by accountants hunched over their ledgers a hundred or more years ago. At the restaurant I asked him, "What's on your mind? Why this sudden lunch?"

He removed his visor and set it gently on the table. "No special reason. I'm hungry, that's all. And I thought I'd stay in touch, see how you're doing."

"I'm all right. I'm getting by. — You look fine. How's the deal for the new gallery going?"

"On schedule," he said brightly. "Next week I'll be closing the gallery."

"*Next week?* You're closing the old place *next week?*"

"I told the people who own the building I'd be leaving. I told them a year ago. No problem."

"But where will you go? Is the new place ready?"

"You mean the place on Newbury Street?" He laughed in what I took to be a purposeful display of his most jovial self. "There's a lot to be done first, beforehand, and it all takes time, especially when so many people are involved — building inspectors, finicky lawyers, expensive architects, real estate agents looking to make a quick fortune."

"You'll have no gallery for months? You'll vanish," I told him.

"No, no, no! The Conti Gallery isn't going to vanish." He leaned forward and said, "The Conti Gallery has a permanent phone number, a fax number, and a website." Now he leaned back and smiled. "And no expenses for these slack months when nobody buys paintings."

"Have you taken the new space? Are you actually there yet?"

"We're ready to go in and disembowel the place, clean it out to the brick walls. I've already hired a crew, Guatemalan immigrants, wonderful people, willing to work hard."

"When do you open on Newbury Street?"

"It will happen on schedule and have we talked about your one-man show? Your opening and the opening of the gallery — the official formal opening, not the preliminary exhibits — will be on the same date. A gala occasion. And before that happy occasion occurs, I want to select a couple of your paintings to show privately to a few buyers, people I've interested in your work — collectors, exceptional people, genuine, very genuine."

I hadn't thought about an exhibit since Leo's last visit. The prospect of a one-man show didn't excite me the way it would have in the past, and neither did the possibility of selling to a collector, even a very genuine collector. But at the same time I didn't like his gliding mention of preliminary exhibits before the gala reception for my works, and a black thought flapped through my mind that maybe the new gallery on Newbury Street was an illusion, a flashy maneuver to keep us painters distracted while Conti the Magician gathered up his goods and dropped though a trapdoor to Switzerland where he had a numbered bank account crammed with money and titles to Boston real estate. I was able to say, "That's great, Leo," and let it go at that.

For lunch, Leo had *feuillité jambon champignons*, a delicate flaky bread sandwich with ham and mushrooms, which was impressive, while I had cold chicken and raw vegetables on a split baguette. Leo talked, or thought out loud, about his getting an additional as-

sistant or, maybe not an assistant but an intern, a really
bright Art History student from, say, Yale or Harvard,
or possibly Princeton, who a few years from now would
write deep articles about painters the Conti Gallery
had promoted. Then he debated with himself whether
it would be exploitive to employ an unpaid intern. We
also talked about same-sex couples having children or,
to be precise, Leo talked about it and I listened, having
no thoughts on the subject, and about politics, where
we agreed that Congress was a dysfunctional mess and
that it would be best to bring a guillotine to the House
of Representatives and start over, and so on to the fi-
nancial mess. I asked had the recession hurt sales. Leo
made a long face and shrugged. "People are cautious
these days, even rich people. What can I do? Have a
fire sale? I have to appear prosperous."

"You've always appeared prosperous to me, Leo."

"Thank you. It's a disguise."

"A very good disguise," I said.

"Did I tell you I'd take care of the brochure? The
entire expense, I'll take care of it."

"No, Leo, you didn't." There had always been some
damn thing I was paying for in my shows at the Conti
Gallery — postcards, a brochure, insurance, advertise-
ments. "You're paying? Tell me about it."

"I see it as an illustrated exhibit catalog. Almost.
Not gaudy," he hastened to add. "Not inflated. Not
overdone. But something rich and fine."

Leo Conti wasn't rich. He was a gallery owner who

loved art, had an eye for talent and worked ceaselessly to promote a certain vision, and he was also a former accountant with an intricate understanding of the gray areas in real estate and tax law, so I can also say he wasn't poor. Over the years I'd heard of a handful of gallery owners who made a lot of money, but I'd seen firsthand that most don't — half of them just get by and the other half go bust inside of five years. Leo was doing well, maybe very well. While we were finishing our coffee, he told me about a young painter he had exhibited a few times in group shows. "The kid's got talent but he's a difficult pain in the ass. Always complaining and asking for an advance. I told him, Give me something I can sell and I'll give you some money. Then the kid informs me about this Manhattan gallery owner who supports his artists when they're broke, gives them cash and a pat on the back. The kid tells me, As a gallery owner, you should cultivate your painters." Leo laughed quietly, reminiscently. "I told the kid, a gallery owner who cultivates his painters that way goes broke. I cultivate buyers."

That was fine by me.

❧

On this sunny day I was walking back to my car in the parking lot of Big Valley Farms, the sky a robin's-egg shade of blue with puffy white clouds here and there, like laundry baskets overfilled with freshly dried bedsheets, and just enough breeze to make the halyard slap against the big flagpole, the same sound we used to hear from the sailboats at anchor in the Merrimack, and I was so lonely, lonely, lonely. I climbed onto the car roof and shouted to the women unloading their shopping carts, I'm dying of loneliness. Rescue me! Rescue me from this terrible loneliness! Then I dropped back into my body, put my groceries in the car and drove home.

❦

I drove to Peasant Bread & Fancy Pastries to see Lucy Dolan. The little bell jingled overhead and she came in from the back room — her hair was wrapped in what looked like the colorful banner of an exotic country and her gold hoop earrings flashed. "Renato! How good to see you!"

"I'm desperate. I need a fancy pastry."

She smiled. "You came to the right place. Right now it's mostly bread, but there are some pastries over here. See?"

There were sugar cookies, fancy cupcakes, a row of Napoleons, then a small tray of ladyfingers, and next to it — "That looks like a tiramisu," I said.

"It is indeed."

"I'll take two. How's business?"

"So far, so good," she said, lifting the tiramisu from behind the glass. Lucy went on to say that she was definitely going to add a small round café table and a chair, or maybe two tables and a couple of chairs, so we

—136—

talked about that, and then about the odor of freshly baked bread which, so far as she could tell, everybody liked. "There was a study they did in France," she told me. "And they found that people became more altruistic when they smelled freshly baked bread."

"I don't believe you."

She smiled. "It's a fact. A scientific fact."

"I want to believe you, but I don't."

"Maybe you're not trying hard enough, Renato."

I laughed. "I'm trying harder than you know."

She told me that the odor of freshly baked bread had such a good effect on people that chemists had come up with a concoction that smelled just like it, and now food stores that got their bread from a bakery located miles away would spray this odor in the air to make people feel more like buying a loaf. "But you haven't told me what you've doing. How have you been?"

"I'm getting by," I said.

"Getting by? Tell me more."

The bell over the door jingled and a woman came in to ask for a dozen sugar cookies. "A baker's dozen," Lucy told her, adding an extra one. It was a pleasure to watch her doing nothing more than chatting with the woman, and the woman left clearly pleased with the exchange of pleasantries. As for me, I wanted to spend the whole afternoon here, bantering with Lucy. We talked about one thing and another until I felt I should leave or I'd make a fool of myself by hanging around. Another woman came in, bought a baguette, went out. I said, "I have to get going."

"Wait, wait! This way, come. Let me show you the table and chair I bought for the store. You can tell me what color to paint them." The back room was warm. The bent-wire chair and circular café table were just inside the rear door. "What do you think?" she asked me.

"Those are perfect," I said. "They look like you snatched them from a Parisian café."

"Actually, they're from Montreal."

"Close enough," I said.

"What colors?"

"How about a luminescent lemon yellow? Bonnard said there's no such thing as too much yellow."

"Be serious."

"Seriously, it's your café and I like what you've done here, and I'm sure you'll paint these the right colors."

"I was thinking, black table, blue chair," she said.

"Perfect."

I figured it was the right moment to leave, so I did. It was a good day, the best in a long while.

❦

So the summer wore on and the days repeated the days of the year before, and each day was like any other. I tried to keep up Alba's many flowerbeds, which had grown to a tangle of weeds, wild grasses, and brittle paper stalks left from the end of last summer, but I didn't know a thing about flowers. My colleague Eloise Carol had retired from the Copley College of Art and was a master gardener, so I phoned her and side-by-side we dug and raked, went out to lunch, then back to the gardens. We had been coworkers but not close because, in addition to her work as a printmaker in everything from lithography to serigraphy, she had written "The Male Gaze as Rape" and other pamphlets about male painters which had set my teeth on edge. "I don't hate men," she once told me, "I hate masculinity." We sweated over the flowerbeds for a week and got along well together, then late on Friday we sat on the porch of her large Victorian house, drank cool wine, and talked some about Alba and then about Helen, Eloise's partner of fifteen years, who had moved out one spring day two years ago, devastating Eloise. "She left me for a younger woman," Eloise said, with a short dry laugh. We watched the sky turn from light blue to pink to violet and debated desire and loss and being old, and when the first tiny stars appeared I drove home, baffled by love and grief and the ways we lived.

❦

Some of my polo shirts needed repair and, as I can't sew to save my life, much less a shirt, I asked Felicia at Café Mondello if she knew anyone who did sewing, but no, she didn't, and neither did Katelin at La Pâtisserie, and when I asked Garland at the Daily Grind, she said, "I'm happy to tell you I haven't sewn a stich since I grew up and left home." But Roxy, who was making a latte for me, pumped her fist in the air, saying, "Hey, I know how to sew." So Roxy (who had quit doing drugs and dumped her boyfriend, and was saving her cash for Culinary Arts school) and I talked, agreed on a price, and the shirts got done.

It's happened before but it's always a rude shock when the pee comes out scarlet with blood, my faithful prostate having been abused by a couple of surgeries. I phoned the urologist's office and spoke to the doctor's assistant, told her I had seen hematuria before, told her I was drinking lots of water and would stop taking my daily aspirin tomorrow morning. "Excellent," she says. "You know the routine — and don't forget to stop the caffeine, stop the alcohol, stop spicy foods, and no chocolate, either." By day three I was peeing urine as clear as a mountain stream and the withdrawal from caffeine had tied my brain in a knot, but by the end of the summer I was back to eating and drinking like my old self. Old in that sentence means old.

I don't know how a person without children lives. Skye and Astrid (or Galaxy, as she wishes) and Fabrizio came by, one family or another almost every month, which was a pleasure while they were here but painful after they'd gone and the house had filled with empty silence again, and no Alba to talk with about the kids, about the way they're living and do they know what they're doing.

Elizabeth Prescott and I had a pleasant lunch and

she gave me her article on Cormac McCormac, which I read later that night. The carefully written profile caught as much of him as an academic article could, I suppose, and reading about Cormac put me in a melancholy mood. Elizabeth and I got together for another lunch and a couple of afternoon coffee meetings, but our conversation never found its way beyond stories about our children and grandchildren or politics and the wars, and we haven't seen each other for a while.

A couple of times I had lunch with Frank Vanderzee who is always good company. He's the same age as my Brizio, give or take a year, and in some ways he reminds me of myself — my younger self, that was — especially as he loves the solitude of painting but also relishes convivial talk with friends deep into the night. We met, Vanderzee and I, a dozen years ago, because he sought me out, which was enormously gratifying to this older painter, especially as I was at the bottom of my career at the time. As for Winona and Gail, they tell me they were pals when Vanderzee met them and all three got along, one step leading to another and another leading to bed. When I met them, they were camped out in Vanderzee's studio in an old industrial building in Boston's South End — Vanderzee, Gail and her two-year-old Azizi, plus Winona and baby Saskia. That was a dozen or fourteen years ago and now they have a house with two fireplaces, a big kitchen, two bedrooms for the kids, two for the adults, and a guest room where I'm invited to spend any weekend I want, which I've not done and probably never will, being as I am old and sad and would feel like a gravestone at the breakfast table.

Andrews, the ophthalmologist, tells me he's very pleased with his handiwork on my eyes. Earlier this year, when he did the surgery to relieve intraocular pressure, he also removed the cloudy lens and inserted a clear plastic one, the same as he'd done a couple of years before in my other eye. I'm now familiar with the basic mechanics of trabeculectomies and cataract surgery. I can also describe, from the patient's perspective, a transurethral resectioning of the prostate, endoscopic gall bladder surgery, endoscopic retrograde cholangio-pancreatography to insert and remove a stent from the billiary duct, and various hernia repairs.

I got around to returning Fletcher's wood clamps. We hooked up for coffee now and again, but I always forgot to bring the clamps. Finally, I put them in my van so the next time we got together I could give them to him. As it happened, Fletch gave a reading from his novel at the Aldus Bookstore, so I went to that and tucked the wood clamps into his Mini Cooper. Mostly I avoid readings. Unlike gallery receptions, which are full of chatter and cheap wine, literary readings are serious affairs where everyone is seated facing the author, like in church or a schoolroom, and some writers, mostly poets, have a lugubrious way of reading, their voices dying at the end of each line. But I liked

Fletch's because when he reads or talks about his book he's so animated, as if his novel was a surprise to him — it *amazes* him — and he always has a table with a big coffeepot and sliced cake or some other confection for us to snack on.

I went out to Nils' place three or four times to help him make a swimming hole in the little stream that runs through his property. Nils and I met years ago as teachers at Copley College of Art, but he taught only half-time, which was what he wanted so that he and his wife Hanna would be at least half-free to go to foreign art festivals, learn to make mandolins, weave cloth, produce computer art — whatever that is — and mosaics. I liked Nils and I liked Hanna, despite her belief that performance art was an art. They never made much money from whatever their art happened to be, but Nils was handy at carpentry and was sought out for restorations by people who had the cash to pay for such things, and for a while Hanna had a fabric shop, then she designed and sewed glittery outfits for rock musicians and dancers, and recently she'd become a costumer for theatrical productions, so they got by pretty well.

About thirty years ago they bought a broken-down dairy farm (no cows) and had been repairing and extending the house ever since. The biggest part was up by the road with half a dozen smaller additions, halls, garages and sheds joined together behind it, one after the other, like railroad cars. The stream that ran through the bottom of their lot was narrow and shallow, but Nils figured if he cut away the bank on both sides and put some big stones where the stream narrowed, he'd have a nice waist-deep pool. So we rolled boulders and carried stones for days and I learned I wasn't as strong as I used to be.

❧

Lucy decided to be called Lucia again, because Lucia went better with Peasant Bread & Fancy Pastries, she said. "Peasants and fancy pastries are European, and Lucia sounds more European than Lucy. — Jacob always called me Lucia. Do you remember?"

"I remember it well," I said. "We all called you Lucia back then."

She smiled, clearly gratified.

"Astrid has two names. She's known as Galaxy in her role as documentary filmmaker."

"Astrid!" She laughed. "Oh, God, we had great fun back then. Your kids were great. *Are* great!"

It was a pleasure to see Lucy, or Lucia, when she laughed, her face brightening, eyes sparkling, though in repose or when focused on a task, you saw the bones beneath the flesh and the fine net of lines around the eyes, which allowed me to pretend I was not this old man being foolish about that much younger woman. Before opening the bakery she had been staying with her friend Alison in Arlington, but now she had found an apartment, one side of a little duplex — "Out here in the country," was the way she put it.

"Out in the country?" I said. "The only country in this town is in a nature preserve."

"Too many trees, not enough people," she told me. She asked what was new in my life and I said nothing was new, absolutely nothing, then she said she was reading a biography of Abigail Adams and asked had I ever read it. I said, "No. But Alba always liked Abigail Adams and knew more about her than she knew about some of her own friends."

"They were a great marriage, Abigail and John," she said.

So we talked about the Adamses and about Jefferson, then Lucia — it's a pleasure to write her name that way — told me how to make hot flip, which was a winter drink in the late 1700s that you heated by taking a hot poker from the fire and quenching it in your tankard of rum, after which we discussed the two small round café tables she now had, and agreed she should paint them black and paint each of the four chairs a different color, the colors being harmonious with each other. As it turned out, I painted the tables and chairs a week or two later. And for the large blank wall, I agreed not to portray God transmitting the spark of life to Adam's limp by means of a loaf of Italian bread. "But I still think it's a good idea," I told her.

❧

You know how when you enter Big Valley Farms the traffic bends you to the right and they've arranged the fruit and vegetable stands in the middle of your pathway, so you walk around and between them, and the other day they had pyramids of yellow grapefruit and oranges and lemons on one side and big bunches of grapes, translucent green and frosted purple, on the other, and further along a mountain of potatoes with snow-white onions in the distance, so next day I bring my camera and, of course, they had switched things around, but it was still interesting and I took some photos. When I got home, I was looking at the speckled yellow pears and glossy red peppers I had bought and I began to wonder if I picked them up simply for their color. I wish I felt like painting. On the other hand, I have more time to prepare dinner and I enjoy the meditative spell of slicing vegetables for a salad or stir-fry or, in winter, vegetable soup. The other day I did the math and I figured you made at least eighteen thousand dinners for us.

❧

Sometimes when I'm dead and it's Alba who's alive, she's at a candlelight dinner with friends and the man seated across from Alba is her companion, a retired naval officer, or it's a summer day and those two are walking together and she's attentive to what he's saying. I know I'm dead and gone, but still I recoil at the scene. The man is one of those restrained, priggish and punctilious heroes from the Jane Austen novels that Alba liked so much.

❦

I was online looking up bread recipes and came across an article about the aroma of baking bread and — *lo and behold!* — it said researchers at a university in Brittany had discovered that the scent of baking bread puts people in an amiable mood and they're more likely to act altruistically. So Lucia wasn't daft — she was right and I was delighted.

❦

One Saturday morning in September, Leo Conti phoned to remind me that he was driving out to select works for the gallery. And, by the way, he was bringing his new intern with him. "She's good. Probably not what you had in mind when I said I was hiring an intern, but very good. And I'm paying her, so she's not really an intern." I remembered Leo telling me he was thinking of getting a brainy graduate from Yale or Harvard or some such place, but I'm sure I never had anything in mind about it.

Later that day his beige Mercedes dove into the ruts of my driveway, came to a jouncing halt and here he was. "I love being close to nature," he announced. Leo was in a stylish hunting vest, the kind with leather-trimmed pockets to hold shotgun shells and a leather patch up front by the shoulder to cushion the rifle butt. "And this is Quincy, my new associate," he said, introducing a woman in her thirties — violet hair hanging below her shoulders, a khaki t-shirt that looked to be made of silk, her left arm illuminated by a sinuous tattoo dense with color, short pants and delicate sandals. The short pants revealed a further tattoo descending her left leg, the empty outline of Art Nouveau scrollwork. Her skin was remarkably white and the tattoo artist must have enjoyed working on it.

Quincy and I shook hands, her straight-on gaze assessing me as I was assessing her. She said, "My daughter won't bother you. She's got a book to read and her guitar, so she can keep herself busy." She was referring to a girl of — I don't know — maybe twelve or thirteen, sitting in the backseat of the Mercedes, watching us.

We all three walked to the barn, Quincy drifting behind us, and I said to Leo, "There's something we have to talk about."

He looked at me. "What do you mean?"

"I painted a lot of these canvases for this barn. They're composed to be seen together, in a certain arrangement, in that space."

"Why are you telling me this?"

"I don't know what you want for the gallery, but a lot of these paintings aren't for sale."

"Renato, I know that. I know it because you've been telling me for five years. That's why I'm going to pick out a group of paintings and you're going to tell me which ones we can offer to those people who are eager to buy your work. Agreed?"

I said I agreed and kept quiet. I wanted an exhibit and at the same time I didn't want to have anything to do with it and, anyway, I felt vaguely disagreeable, maybe because of Conti's assistant, and pissed at myself for feeling that way toward Conti who, after all, liked my work and sold it.

As we came along the old orchard, Leo picked one of the apples. "Is this safe to eat?" he asked me.

"It's an apple, Leo. People have been eating them for centuries."

"This one looks kind of wormy."

"That worm would never eat the apple if it wasn't a healthy apple. Eat from the other side."

While we walked, he turned the apple this way and that and looked skeptical. "I'll eat it later," he said, pushing it into his pocket.

I shoved open the barn door and we went inside. There was plenty of light pouring in from the high windows, but I showed him where the light switches were if he wanted to use them. I went upstairs to the loft and opened the studio door, then went down and told Leo he could look at anything. He was already moving some of the stretchers around. His assistant hung back, shifting from foot to foot, starting to bite a fingernail, then abruptly jamming her hand into her pocket. I told her to take a look around, make herself at home. She responded with a fleeting smile which was more like a nervous tic. I doubted she was the Art History student from Harvard or Yale that

Leo had been looking for. I asked her where she had studied.

"Vermont," she said. "And Maine," she added.

What kind of an answer was that? "Those are good states," I said, after searching for something to say. "Yup, good New England states."

I told Leo I was going back to the house and would return in a half-hour or so.

Quincy's daughter had opened the car's rear doors and was sitting inside, reading. She glanced up and watched me as I went by, so I stopped to ask did she want anything, maybe a glass of water or something to eat. She hesitated, then said she had already eaten lunch, thank you anyway. I thought to ask her what she was reading, but decided against it, went inside and made myself a cup of coffee.

I had been working for thirty years to get my paintings back on Newbury Street and I wanted to get this exhibit in the new Conti Gallery on that same street, and it didn't matter to me that there might be better venues somewhere else in Boston — I wanted my work on that street — and at the same time I didn't care piss about the paintings or the exhibit. Alba had said those were good works, great works, and she had lived the life we lived, never having an extra dollar, so I could paint, and it was up to me to make sure we got this goddamn exhibit. After the show I could lie down to die, because I wasn't going to paint another canvas because there wasn't anyone to show it to. I finished the coffee, washed out the cup and the coffeepot, and headed outside.

Quincy's daughter watched from the car as I went by and I got to the apple trees before I turned around and walked back and said, "Your mother's looking at some paintings in the barn, which is where I'm going and you can come along, too, if you want." She had the guitar in her lap, which she set carefully aside before hopping out.

We walked along. I asked her, "Would you rather read or play the guitar?"

She frowned a moment, thinking about it. "I'm not too good on the guitar. I'm just learning. I like to read, too. I like to read mysteries. But I'm not so good on the guitar."

Her sunshine-blonde hair was pulled back to a short ponytail held in place with a rubber band, and she wore a dazzling white t-shirt with slight bumps there and there to indicate her breasts.

"I bet you play fine," I told her.

She smiled and made a lovely delicate fingering gesture in the air. "I'm improving, I think."

When we reached the barn, Leo was standing outside, scanning the sky. "You got fantastic clouds out here. Look at those things. And I saw a hawk!"

Quincy's daughter walked quickly ahead to her mother who was deep inside, crouched in front of one of the paintings, writing in a notebook.

"So you've met Sylvan," Leo told me. I must have looked blank, because he added, "Quincy's daughter."

"Yes, nice kid. And you say Quincy is a good assistant, or associate or something?"

"You sound doubtful, Renato. She's learning. She
doesn't know your work the way I do but she's a quick
study. Very bright. — She went to Harvard."

"She told me Maine and Vermont. Harvard's in
Massachusetts."

"She was at Harvard for a year. Practically a year.
A semester and a half, anyway. Then she took a break.
Later she went to a couple of those colleges where
you go for a week and they tell you what to study and
then you go off to where you came from and study and
write papers. Which means she's self-motivated and
has lots of initiative. She's connected to the art world,
maybe not exactly what you and I would call mature
painters, but the coming art world. Also, she has a certain refinement and can talk well to buyers. — Good
family background."

Quincy had finished her note-taking and now
mother and daughter were headed our way.

"Listen," Leo said, lowering his voice. "This has
been a learning experience for her. I'll come out here
again without her and we'll talk, you and me. We'll
go over the paintings together. This is going to be a
great exhibit."

Quincy came up, now wearing eyeglasses or, more
precisely, a single eyeglass — one of the lenses was
missing and the hinge to the temple piece was ban-
daged with adhesive tape.

"I hope you like what you saw," I said.

"Oh, yes. Leo gave me photographs of your work to study and I looked forward to seeing the actual paintings. I think gallery-goers can benefit from seeing the works of the previous generation, the earlier painters. It provides historical context for the contemporary art scene." She went on a while more, but by then my head was echoing badly, blotting out whatever else she said. When she had finished, I said, "Oh. Well. Thanks. I never thought of it that way."

￼

Luci or Lucy or Lucia, whichever way she spelled her name I liked her — in fact, I liked her a lot — and though I have more vanity and foolishness in me than most men, I don't have enough to delude myself about her and me. Conversation was easy with her and we had dinner together now and again, but she evaded coming to my home, perhaps to save me from a grotesque blunder, and we ate only in restaurants where she insisted on splitting the bill. One Wednesday she told me she was "getting away from it all, going to Montreal with a friend" for the weekend. And one Sunday morning I drove to her place on a whim to take her out for breakfast, but when I turned into the parking place behind her apartment, the guest slot was occupied by a rusted van from Boudreau Electric that had snuggled up close to her little Toyota, so without stopping I swung around and headed home.

❦

Leo Conti drove out here to make a final selection of paintings for the show and ended up choosing the same ones Alba had told me would go best at the gallery. Conti and I argued over one painting, a four-by-six that Alba always said should be darker. I told her, I don't do darker than that. Now Leo was saying the same damn thing, Make it darker, make it darker. You began it dark, he says, so make it darker. I told him, I like color and I'm good at it and black is the absence of color so do you want me to punch a goddamn hole in the canvas? And he says, I didn't say black, I said *darker*. Then he drove off with two frescos I should have smashed long ago, but he thinks they'll interest a buyer he has in mind.

❦

Katia and I had lunch a couple of times as she crisscrossed Eastern Massachusetts, looking for a church where she and the parish were a good match, then one morning she phoned to tell me she had found what she was looking for. She said she felt like celebrating and wanted to take me out for lunch. "That's great," I said, "But I'm supposed to meet Leo Conti at noon in Boston, so he can show me the new gallery." Katia asked, Where's the gallery? and I said, On Newbury Street, if I can believe him, and Katia said, Wonderful! Because after you've inspected the gallery we can have lunch on Newbury.

And, in fact, the gallery was on Newbury, just as Leo had promised. The sidewalks were flooded with people and the street looked narrower than I had remembered, the shops smaller, but there was an excitement about this parade of outdoor cafés, fancy boutique clothiers, expensive trinket shops and pricy art galleries. The interior of the Conti Gallery had been peeled away to the brick walls, the floors had been refinished and a loose skein of electrical lines dangled from sockets in the ceiling. "I'm impressed, Leo."

"I thought you would be."

"When will the gallery be ready?"

"For you? November."

I looked around, wondering how my paintings would look in this space. Suddenly I missed Alba so much it hurt and I almost winced. Leo was watching me and waiting. "This is good, Leo," was all I said. "Very good."

As we were leaving, Leo reached up and patted my back, saying, "You're going to be all right. This is going to be great. And remember, I'm taking care of everything."

We crossed the street and walked to the Café Boul'Mich, a pleasant stroll, the air being cool and the noonday sun just warm enough, and we stood there talking about his gallery expenses until I saw Katia approaching — a big wave from her, then greetings all around, after which Leo headed off, and Katia and

I found a table at the café. I had forgotten what it was like to sit at a café table with throngs of people walking by and for a moment I simply soaked in it. "I remember meeting him at some of your exhibits," she said about Leo. "But I think he had a lot of hair or was taller or something. How did the new gallery look?"

"Unfinished but good. Surprisingly good, in fact. It makes me feel like celebrating, so let me buy you lunch."

"My new church looks good, too, so let me buy you lunch, which was our plan."

We gave the waiter our orders and I asked Katia about her new parish.

"More intellectual than most," she said. "The retiring pastor was known for his brains, not his piety or good fellowship, and despite his reputation for intelligence, people come from two or three towns away to listen to him. The congregation — I think, I hope — is the kind I've been looking for. It sounds good, and at my age this is going to be my last position."

"At your age? Are you pretending to be old? You certainly don't look the part."

Katia laughed. "It's the chaste life I lead. My youth and beauty last forever because my heart is pure. No sins, no wrinkles."

You need to know something about Katia. She married her college boyfriend a month after graduating from UMass and followed that by graduating pregnant from Union Theological Seminary, but as soon as the baby was born she and her husband split. "Because at the seminary I discovered there were two things I enjoyed and was truly interested in, theology and sex. And I had intimations that these were more than interests, they were passions, and if we stayed married I'd betray him and make his life miserable and I didn't want to do that. He was a decent guy, you know. I got pregnant because I'd already had a miscarriage and I wanted a baby and I told him so and, after all, even though we had called it quits we were still sleeping in the same bed, the only difference being that our sex life was better than when we thought we were stuck with each other. He loved working on Wall Street, theology bored him, and he certainly wasn't ready to be a father, so it was best for both of us." That's what she told Alba and me.

Katia didn't intend to become a pastor when she entered the seminary; she simply loved theology and when her son turned four, Katia began a new course of study at Union Theological. We didn't see much of her during those years, but from her occasional notes and visits we understood that she was indulging her passions. We were surprised, though maybe we shouldn't have been, when she told us she had decided to become a pastor. "Obviously it can't be Catholic or Episcopalian and I'm not interested in anything less than Lutheran, but that's too confining — they're all too confining — so it's nondenominational, and I know that sounds weird, but I think I can do that. — And I love you for being so patient," she told us.

Here and now at the Café Boul'Mich, we ate lunch and talked about her new parish, about what Katia said were "all these intellectuals in Eastern Massachusetts, some of them — many of them — believe, or have a desire to believe, that there's something beyond the material world they deal with every day."

I asked were they mostly younger or mostly older.

She smiled. "Mature is the word I prefer. Most of them are mature. But there are others, of course, people who describe themselves as not religious but spiritual. Spiritual is a word that leaves a bad taste in my mouth," she added.

"We never understood how you arrived at your faith, or what kind of faith it was and, I admit, well, we didn't have the nerve to ask."

The waiter came by, flashed the dessert menu at us and confided that the crème brûlée was irresistible. We resisted and ordered espressos.

Katia said, "You two were probably wondering how I could be bedding this one and that one and be a woman of faith. I wondered that too, once in a while. I'm lucky I survived my own foolishness. But I knew there was a God. As far back as I can remember I knew there was a God. Knowing whether or not I had a calling, a true vocation — that was a puzzle, but I was willing to take that chance."

"We knew you had this natural belief in God — it was such a rare thing — but we never knew what you'd do next."

"Neither did I. I mean, I was still sleeping around, so why would God call me to religious life? To get me to stop? I don't think so. I think I'm just slow at understanding who I am. Eric and I were together long before I realized I was in love with him." Katia was referring to the man she had been living with for the last several years. "It took me a while to know I was called. I'm slow. But I go pretty far," she added, with a slight smile.

I laughed. "I remember you were celibate for a while."

"Ah, you do remember! Yes, when Theo turned thirteen and until he went off to college. It wasn't so bad. In fact, it was good."

"I can't say I ever had faith," I said. "Sometimes I believed, but it wasn't a strongly held belief, or maybe it never got to being a belief at all. When I was first in love with Alba — not when we were kids, but when we were in our twenties and found each other again — for days, for weeks, I believed in God. Everything was so stunningly right and beautiful. Actually, it wasn't so much a belief in God as it was a surge of good feelings for the whole world, the universe, an overflow of love toward everyone, including God."

"Oh, I *like* that."

"Everything's gone now," I said. "I believe in nothing."

She looked at me with those same steady, interested eyes she had as a kid, at last saying, "That's understandable."

We fell silent and watched the jumbled stream of people passing by. After a while, Katia said, "When I realized I was in love with Eric, my next thought was how devastated I'd be if anything happened to him. The world would be empty. I don't know, I can't imagine — I mean, I don't want to imagine how I'd feel."

The waiter arrived with our coffee and the bill which he placed with a flourish squarely between us, then off he went.

"You believe in God and I understand that," I said. "I don't think that's a weird belief. It makes sense to me. But who, or what, *is* this God with a capital G?"

Katia hesitated. "If I say God is the creator of heaven and earth, the seas and all things in them, will you be mad at me?"

I had to smile. "No. I won't be mad at you."

"And if I go beyond that and start listing the attributes of God, it gets rather scholastic and, well —"

I broke in, saying, "It wasn't right, Alba's dying. It wasn't right. I was in a rage about that. And I will be forever."

And Katia, all along knowing my mind, said, "Some people would hate God for that. Or they might hate a pastor, thinking she represented God, when actually —"

"I just wanted to die, that's all. I tried to will myself to death."

"The rest of us are happy you failed. And I'm particularly grateful you're right here at this table having coffee with me. You've kept going." She hesitated, then said, "Do you mind if — Can I ask you — What do you believe in that gets you out of bed every morning?"

"I don't know. I don't know much these days. And the more I think about these things, the less I know. I know Alba loved me. I believe in Alba."

I sounded stupid even to me. We drank our coffee and watched the people flowing past, this way and that, and at times overflowing into the street.

"I hope you get back to painting," Katia said. "It may be your calling."

"You're kind to say so."

She smiled. "You're probably tired of hearing me say I love and admire you."

I laughed. "No. Not at all."

It was a good lunch and a fine autumn day and Alba would have enjoyed the three of us being at the Café Boul'Mich on Newbury Street.

∾

After my shower I was trimming my horny toenails, going over this body in the clean morning sunlight, pressing a tender area that hides a femoral hernia, finding a cyst in my groin, a numb passage along my foot, spots of scaly keratosis on my shoulder and wild sprouting hairs anyplace. Old me has become one of those whales you see heave up through tons of sea, their bodies patchy with ancient barnacles; they break

into the air for a moment, fins spreading out like use-
less wings, then they crash down and slide under and
disappear. I crave the lovemaking we used to do. No
woman finds me attractive. I know what you're saying,
and I'm grateful for it, but you're the only one who
ever thought so.

☙

Leo Conti had wanted an artist's statement for the
exhibit catalog, a brief paragraph, he said, and I had
said, Yes, sure, and tossed the crumpled notion into
some corner of my cluttered mind and forgot about
it, because it was too much work and, besides, the
paintings were the goddamn statement. A couple of
weeks later, Conti's associate, the one with violet hair,
Quincy, turned up at my front door with a carryall
under her arm and her daughter by her side, saying
that Conti had sent her to get the statement from me
because, she asserted, he had asked me for it a month
ago and there was a deadline.

I told her to come in and asked would she like a coffee and would Sylvan like some hot apple cider. "The
paintings don't need an explanation," I said.

"It's not an explanation about the paintings," Quincy tells me. "It's about you."

"I'm not going to explain me."

She hesitated a moment and was about to say something, so I said to Sylvan, "I'll make you a mug of hot
apple cider with a cinnamon stick in it. Follow me."

Sylvan followed me and Quincy followed Sylvan, so we were in the kitchen now where Quincy opened her carryall on the table, telling me, "I have statements you made for other exhibits and also interviews you gave that might help you."

"I'm sure I was never so crazy as to explain myself."

She had dumped papers and magazine clippings onto the table and looked up to say, "In an interview you gave a dozen years ago you said you painted to give people solace for being human."

"That was a dozen years ago. I was young and hopeful."

"You were seventy," she informs me.

"Oh, to be seventy again."

"I thought we could start there and add to it," she says.

I poured a mug of apple cider for Sylvan and gave her a stick of cinnamon to drop into it, then I put the mug into the microwave.

Quincy was persistent, meaning we two sat at the kitchen table and debated the merits of artists' statements while her daughter, who had taken her mug of hot cider to the front room, looked through the shelf of books left behind by my children and grandchildren as they grew up. There was nothing Quincy could pry out of me because I had nothing to say. After an hour, she gave up, dropped the clippings back into her carryall, and went to the front room to get her daughter, who was seated cross-legged on the floor with an open book in her hand, studying the map of some magical kingdom that lay unfolded in her lap. "Put the book back and say thank-you and goodbye to Mr Stillamare," Quincy told her.

❦

You probably don't remember, but I one day caught you by the wrist as you were passing by in the kitchen, caught you by surprise, and you turned and asked, "Are you going to take me to your pirate ship?" I don't know why I remembered that just now, but I did. That was so long ago.

❦

Late one fall afternoon Fletcher and I were raking leaves at his place and talking about how when we were kids our families used to rake leaves out to the street and then burn them in the gutter, so the delicately sharp odor of burning leaves became the scent of fall. "Now they don't allow it in any of these towns, not anymore," he said. We missed that odor and we talked about the smell of torn grass and damp soil that came to your nose when you were scrimmaging on the football field, and how cold you got walking home after practice with the dark coming on. I remember that part, but I don't recall how the talk got from there to books and the last chapters of novels. I know I asked him, "Why do novels always come to a satisfying conclusion, no matter what's happened, no

matter what dreadful things have happened along the
way, there's a sense of rightness at the end? That's not
the way life is."

"That's why novels are called fictions," Fletch said.
"A novel isn't life, it's fiction."

"I thought a novel was supposed to reflect life. My
uncle Zitti liked to say that a novelist was like a man
carrying a big mirror down the road, so it reflects everything — the blue sky overhead and the muddy road
underfoot."

"I think that's from Stendhal."

"Ah, zio Zitti." I laughed. "He loved Stendhal. He
couldn't bear to think of Stendhal as French and always referred to him as a displaced Italian."

"Stendhal was crazy about Italy," said Fletch. "Maybe your uncle was right."

Then we heard Fletch's Kate calling and turned to
see her silhouetted in the tall yellow rectangle of the
open front door. "Dinner's ready," she said. "How can
you guys see what you're doing out there? It's already
dark. Come in, come in."

We dragged the loaded tarpaulin to the street and
dumped the leaves in the gutter where the town could
vacuum them up. As we were walking back toward the
house, Fletch says, "I think that sense of rightness at
the end of a story is like the resolution at the end of
a piece of music. Even the blues or a tragic symphony
has that resolution. It doesn't mean everything turned
out all right."

"It just means it's over," I said.

"Yes, that's it."

Then we went in and had dinner.

☙

I bought vegetables today to make soup — I start with diced tomatoes and I don't use stock — but when I got home and laid the vegetables on the counter I was struck again by the colors — the yellow of the squash is really boastful, and there's the cool celery green and the harsh hue of the carrots and so on. I get into a restful, meditative calm when I cut up vegetables, like I was preparing to paint again, but first I had to slice up a batch of primary colors. It looked so good in the pot that before I ladled it out I took a photo, thinking you should see it — the craziness never goes away. I've done some line drawings and maybe I'll do some work in color.

☙

A week ahead of the exhibit, Leo Conti sent me twenty copies of the exhibit catalog. He had outdone himself. It was extraordinary — a big, flat paperbound catalog printed on deliciously heavy glazed paper, like the pages of the art book my father had bought for our home when I was a kid. That volume was my first course in art history and I loved the big color prints and the sound of the pages sliding heavily upon each other. Now here's the catalog of *Works by Renato Stillamare* at the Conti Gallery on Newbury Street in Boston, Massachusetts. It reproduces almost every painting in the show and has not only a running text around the paintings, but also an additional two pages about the artist's oeuvre through the decades. And look at old Renato now as he takes an armful of catalogs to the barn and climbs the stairs to his studio, dropping some in his haste, so he can bring them to the shelf where the photographs of Alba wait, where he can lay a catalog open in front of her — the old bastard is sobbing now — saying, *Look, Alba. See? We made it. We got the exhibit on Newbury Street. We did it. See? We did it.*

❦

The show was a success. The paintings looked good, the gallery was almost spacious enough, and there I was (smiling, warm-hearted, appreciative), engaging with everyone, not moving around much because friends were coming up to offer congratulations and to see for themselves if Stillamare had more or less recovered, because he went absolutely and completely, you know, *crazy*, after his wife died. The inner man was astonished at what the outer shell was capable of. Skye and Eric had driven down to my place and then to the gallery where Skye stood beside me to maneuver people this way or that, and when I hadn't caught a name she'd repeat it along with a phrase to remind me who was who. Astrid and Weston arrived at the same time as Brizio and Heather — meaning we were all together now, except their mother wasn't here.

Among my friends there was Zoe and Emerson, of course, and Zocco and his wife (still limping a bit), Avalon (in a shimmering peacock-blue dress slashed up to her thigh, because Alba had once praised her for wearing it) and Sebastian, Nils and Hanna, Scott and fragile Rachel, George Agathos (crackers and cheese in one hand, a glass of Chablis in the other, saying, "You have exceeded yourself!") and his Io, Fletcher and Kate, Lucia and her friend Alison, and others I hadn't seen in a while, like Scanlon and his wife who drove up from Connecticut, and the Goetemanns from Gloucester, plus a number of painters who had regular shows at the galley and were required to attend out of politeness.

The scattering of early-comers thickened up and the gallery grew pleasingly crowded. Quincy (high-heel shoes, trim gray suit, her violet hair held back by a silver clasp) introduced me to a trio she said were "really awesome painters" — a young man who had a degree from Copley College where I used to teach, another in a World War II airman's leather jacket, and a young African-American woman with a faint British accent in a striking red Maasai dress and jewelry. They were a decent bunch and after their polite remarks about my work (including the fifty-year-old witticism that Stillamare paints nudes as if they were landscapes and landscapes as if they were nudes) we relaxed and talked about studio space and the high cost of everything. More and more of the people were unknown to me, which was a good sign, especially when Leo introduced them to me.

Leo had chosen an authentic appearance for himself this evening — no wig, his head bald as a cannonball but slightly tanned, a plain gray suit and, peeking above his jacket's breast pocket, a pair of reading glasses as a friendly and informal touch. He wouldn't be doing any reading tonight, but he'd use the folded glasses to point out this or that when talking.

I caught a glimpse of Winona and Gail, and later Vanderzee turned up. My first exhibit with Leo had been a sprawling affair in East Cambridge and halfway through the evening Vanderzee had left, returning with his clarinet and three friends to play Dixieland until the gallery was a wreck of empty wine bottles and crumpled paper cups. Now Vanderzee shook my hand, looked around at the long dresses and money, and said, "Good crowd. Too bad I didn't bring my band."

Leo Conti introduced me to Kenneth Parkman, telling me, "Kenneth is Quincy's father." Kenneth Parkman, a tall middle-aged man with a receding hairline, shook my hand.

"Quincy's a remarkable young woman," I told him.

Parkman nodded slightly, rather thoughtfully it seemed to me. "She has an interest in art," he told me.

"She appears to have an instinct for it, a natural talent," I said.

"One can only hope so," he said, smiling. After a

slight hesitation, he said, or asked, "You have children."

"Yes, and all three are here." I was about to introduce Skye, but she was in an animated conversation with a couple of people.

Parkman had looked about to say something on the subject of children, but glancing around he now said, "This is a fine exhibit, very fine." He turned slightly to the woman who had joined him, bringing her forward, saying "This is Moira, Quincy's mother."

We shook hands and she said, "My granddaughter was delighted with the book you sent her."

"A book?" I didn't know what she was talking about, then half a second later I realized the granddaughter was Sylvan. "Oh, yes! She had been reading it at my place — it belonged to my daughter — so when I came across a new copy I thought I'd send it along."

After we had exchanged a few more pleasantries, they drifted off. The party hummed along and Leo reappeared at my elbow, murmuring, "A gentleman who made a purchase at the advanced viewing is here. That's him, talking with Quincy. He wants to meet you, so let's go to my office."

We trailed Quincy who was already steering the man toward Leo's office. As usual, Leo had given certain buyers a look at the paintings a day or two early, so when the gallery opened this evening a handful of paintings had a handsome red dot beneath them to announce they'd already been sold. Leo had told me that an up-and-coming real estate trader, Mr Somebody, had bought the big semiabstract landscape. In the office we shook hands and I played my artist's role rather well, I thought, but when it was time for me to bow myself away, Leo tells me, "We're not through yet," then we push into the crowded gallery, a photographer appears out of thin air, and as people begin to turn our way, Leo puts the red dot by the painting and the photographer takes a dozen shots of the Real Estate Patron of the Arts, plus Leo Conti and the artist. I detest these stupid stunts. The buyer would really like da Vinci to paint baby Jesus surrounded by the three wise men, plus the Patron Himself, bringing gifts.

So now I told Skye I wanted a glass of goddamned wine. She took my arm, saying, Don't mutter that way, somebody might hear you, then she walked me to the table and asked, Do you want a glass of goddamned red or goddamned white? I said white and asked her did she think the exhibit was going well. And she said, "Of course it's going well. It's terrific."

Later, Astrid came by and told me, "I saw that camera business. You should rethink not letting me make a movie of one of your gallery exhibits. As part of a documentary, you know."

"Didn't we have this conversation before?"

"You gave me the wrong answer before," she said.

Wine was in my veins, I was feeling expansive and I talked with Brizio and Heather, maybe for too long. Twenty minutes earlier the gallery had been so jammed and warm that a few couples had slipped out-

EUGENE MIRABELLI

side, lingering on the broad stone steps to chat and breathe the cold night air, but now the crowd was thinning away. Spaces were growing larger, emptier, like after Alba's memorial service. Quincy had taken off her jacket, revealing her sleeveless blouse and the brightly colored tattoo that swirled down her left arm, and now she began to clear the table of cheese platters and wineglasses. On the drive back home, Skye and Eric assured me it had been an excellent show, a great exhibit. At home I was still too accelerated to go to sleep, so I made myself a cup of hot cocoa and sat a long time at the kitchen table, waiting, though I knew Alba couldn't tell me my paintings were great, and I couldn't tell her she had been the most beautiful woman in the room tonight.

☙

There are stupid passages in Lucretius that had me scribbling furiously in the margin. He says we're nothing but atoms that disperse when we die, and therefore death is nothing to us, and having reasoned his way to that point, he says we're now free to live like gods. But it's precisely this erasing of the self that we dread. The gods are immortal and we are not, and no, we are not free to live like gods. We die. We don't want to be dispersed or dissolved into the void, we don't want to lose each other. Death was nothing to Lucretius because he never loved and never grieved.

Take those lines where he tells us that often when

a calf is slaughtered at the altar, the calf's bereaved mother — and "mother" is the word he uses — the bereaved mother wanders around, searching for her calf's familiar footprints, filling the woods with her moans, and when she returns to their stall she's pierced with longing for her calf. The passage is famous among classical scholars. But Lucretius doesn't write so much as one tender hexameter about human loss, which grief he treats with chilly reason.

The man doesn't understand people. He wrote two or three hundred lines on sexual passion, all with detachment, irony or mockery. His women are manipulating bitches, the men deluded, and those couples who enjoy each other he compares to a pair of stuck dogs — the poor hound, having mounted his hot bitch, has thrust in but can't pull back out. Lucretius is curious about everything (magnets, the growth of civilization, wet dreams, whatever) — well, so am I, and I admire him for that, but grudgingly.

His description of frenzied lovemaking is as precise as everything else he writes about. He tells us how lovers entangle, press and rub against each other, greedy mouth upon mouth. And even when they've satisfied their cravings and lie melted by the heat of their passion, it's only for a short time and "the hunger comes back, the frenzy and madness return." It's all in vain, he says. They can't wholly embrace or dissolve "or penetrate or be absorbed, body into body" — and, he says, "that's what they appear to be trying to do." Yes,

Lucretius, that's what they're trying to do. But being Lucretius and literal minded, he thinks it impossible.

My friend Mike Bruno used to say that orgasms take place not down there, but in the brain. According to Mike, the tributary nerves carry only simple signals, a little vocabulary of sensations, to the spinal cord, and that bundle of signals speeds to the brain where it's parsed for meaning in the context of everything else that's going on up there, and it's the *meaning* that causes the explosion, sending messages of gratitude back to the provinces, even to the soles of your feet. I don't know if he was right or wrong — Mike was an art critic by trade and had theories about a lot of things. As for me, I can't paint and simultaneously theorize about painting, and the same goes for me and lovemaking.

But Alba and I did sometimes talk about it, awkward and hesitant even years into marriage, just the two of us at the end of the day, the children asleep upstairs. I remember a conversation that began one hot summer evening — I know it was summer because as we got deeper into it I shut the windows so our voices wouldn't carry in the humid stillness of the night — we began to talk about what it was we were doing, this or that or the other, and what it possibly meant, when we made love. In ways that Lucretius could never understand, it's possible to completely embrace or penetrate or be absorbed or dissolve, body into body. And when your beloved has gone, absolutely gone, you feel that half your body has been ripped away, and though you appear whole to everyone, you know you are not.

❦

What I'm trying to do is to give it the sense that you're not there. Remember how you said old Fitzhugh Lane could paint silence? I'm trying to paint absence. I'm hoping the slant and color of light as it rakes across, just touching the perfume bottles, the little jewelry box, your comb, the seashell holding your earrings, and the chamber stick with no candle — I hope it works. I'm not including the big mirror, but instead a high blank wall where the mirror should be. I'm hoping it doesn't look like a neat bureau expecting someone. If I've done it right, it shows you're not here.

❦

One day I was checking the garden fence where the snow was drifted deep and I heard something flutter this way and that in your rhododendron bush, and then a cardinal flew out and landed on the fence post, maybe three feet from me. And you know how cautious those cardinals are. She tilted her head to get a full look at me but didn't fly off, and I thought maybe this is the same cardinal that flew around us when Astrid was looking for a sign from you. Now the cardinal flew to the next fence post and looked at me again, so I went there and waited, wondering what this meant. The sun was high and there was nothing here but us two in this dead garden filled with dazzling snow. Then she flew back to the first post and hopped around to watch me again. So I walked back and watched and waited, and when she was ready she flew up, high up over the empty trees and away.

❦

I received a letter from the New Arts Alliance announcing that in recognition of my work in the visual arts they would be honored to present me with their Biennale Award, on such and such a day in April. I assumed they'd made a mistake. I'd become a member fifty or more years ago when the Alliance was a small gang of insurgent countercultural painters living around Boston. Over the years it grew into a New England regional organization and, though I still gave them a yearly donation, I had let my membership lapse long ago — the revolution was over and the good guys had lost.

I phoned Leo and told him about the award. "Congratulations. And why are you surprised? This is new youth recognizing old youth," he said. I wrote to the New Arts Alliance to express my thanks for the honor of being a recipient of their prestigious award. Apparently they had not made a mistake because the president, Howard Chi, sent me a letter outlining the history of the New Arts Alliance Biennale Award, given every two years for the past twenty years, which was news to me, and I learned that, starting five years ago, the award was presented to two artists at the same ceremony, a "distinguished painter, such as yourself," wrote Chi, and an "emerging artist, such as Esiankiki Fields," who would be honored along with me this year. I had never come across him or her. The prize is a modest sum of money and a small silver Revere bowl.

I hadn't been to a meeting of the New Arts Alliance in thirty years, but Skye drove us to Boston, found a parking space, and stayed by my side, more or less. I was astonished by how young everyone was. There were a few familiar faces — Leo Conti, of course, had received an invitation, and Zocco was a member of the Alliance so he was there, too, with his wife, as was Vanderzee with Gail and Winona. Quincy was a familiar face, her violet hair radiating around her head as if electrified, and I recognized the young painter who had been wearing the World War II airman's jacket at my exhibit. It was a good crowd and there were some bald heads and white beards, but it looked like I was the oldest person in the room.

Two easels stood at the front of the room, one holding a canvas by Esiankiki Fields and the other holding one of mine. Before giving the awards, Howard Chi made a speech, a historical tour through my career with quotes along the way from reviews and interviews, all of which must have come from Quincy's research. The speech was mercifully short, but even before it ended it began to sound rather like an obituary

— specifically, my obituary. I had started to sweat, so it was a relief when he began his remarks about Esiankiki Fields. Fields turned out to be the young African-American woman in a red Maasai dress that Quincy had introduced to me at my show a while back. This evening she was in a red sweater and black pants and wore Maasai earrings with colored beads and dangling coins, a good-looking woman.

After the awards ceremony had broken up, drinks were available, including bourbon, for which I was grateful, and it felt good to relax, have a drink with Vanderzee and his wives, and Zocco, and a handful of others I hadn't seen in years. Esienkiki caught my eye and came over to thank me for having told the Alliance to add my award money to hers. I said I remembered our conversation in the Conti Gallery about the cost of rentals and studio space. And I told her I admired her painting, especially the colors, which was true. As we talked, I learned that her mother had been a Maasai schoolteacher and her father a BBC newsman, which accounted for her slight British accent. She asked about my background and was there a difference between Sicilians and Italians. I laughed and told her, "They say Sicilians are Africans trying to be Italians." I was having a pretty good time.

On the drive home it was easy to sit quietly beside Skye and watch the lights of the city streaming past, then the lights rippling slowly on the inky-black Charles River and, at last, the miles of dark highway. I said, "I wonder how much Quincy helped get me this prize. She knows those people."

"You got the prize because you deserve it. Quincy doesn't control the New Arts Alliance."

I thought about that for a while and wished I knew what Alba would say about tonight. My mind wandered. I told Skye I didn't drive much at night. She said night driving didn't bother her. We lapsed into silence. Then later, I said, "Do you think it sounded like they were giving me a lifetime achievement award?"

"Maybe. You've achieved a lot, after all."

"It sounded like an end-of-life prize," I said.

"No it didn't.

"It sounded like an obituary."

"You're being morbid," she said.

"I'm talking about what it sounded like. My life isn't over. I'm not through," I added.

"Of course you're not through."

For a while I thought of one smart thing after another to tell her, but then I thought better of it and let myself drift along with the night.

❦

Whenever it slips my mind that I'm mortal, my body comes up with an ailment to remind me. Pneumonia can do that.

❦

I came across Shannon behind the coffee bar in a café in Harvard Square! It was good to see her again. She had gained back her weight, looked fine, and had a gold ring on the fourth finger of her left hand. "Look at that," I said, and she said, "That? That's a wedding ring."

"You married Fitz," I said.

"Who else?"

"Congratulations to you both. That's so great."

"It's not all roses. But we're good," she added.

We talked a while and I learned that Fitz was working for an older guy and they repaired washers and dryers. He's quick and can learn anything, Shannon told me. I asked did she like working at this café and was it any good. She said the pay was all right and she got benefits, and as for the customers, "People are the same arrogant douchebags and dickheads the world over."

"And this has changed," I said, holding her arm where the tattooed snake coiled down toward her hand. New words ran along both sides of the snake. "Can I read it?"

Shannon turned her arm and I read *If love could have saved you, you would have lived forever.*

"That's for Robert," she said. "I got it done a couple of weeks before Fitz and I got married."

"That's beautiful. And Fitz is a lucky man. I hope you both live forever."

I can't help it. I'm moved by things like that.

❦

I didn't get around to clearing the vegetable garden until October. I yanked out the stakes, pulled up the withered tomato plants, turned over the soil, then planted three rows of garlic and covered them with a blanket of dead leaves. Maybe next spring I'll plant the usual vegetables, but probably not. It's no fun doing this without you — the same reason I don't tap the sugar maples anymore. There are a lot of things I thought I liked, but it turns out what I liked was doing those things with you. Anyway, this frees up some time. It took me seventy years to learn how to paint so I might as well use every damned day I have left.

❦

I didn't reread Dante, not his claustrophobic epic and certainly not his insipid love poetry, having had enough of that allegorizing sourpuss from my uncle Zitti in my twenties, and from my friend Mike Bruno in my thirties. Mike not only wrote books on art and pornography (and another on cheeses), he was also a great reader of Dante and though I loved Mike I could never love Dante. But a lot of us liked to listen to Mike talk about Dante. One summer night Alba and I drove around to Mike's place to celebrate Nixon's impeachment; the door was ajar, so we knocked and walked in and heard Mike's basso profundo from upstairs, reciting Dante, and when we got up there, yes, there he

EUGENE MIRABELLI

was, sitting up in bed wearing only his eyeglasses, a huge volume of Dante open in his lap, Pam on one side with a plate of cold chicken, and Clarissa on the other with a bottle of wine — all three naked as the day they were born — my own Mike Bruno, now dead twenty years and more.

❦

Alba always liked that poem by John Donne that begins —

> *When my grave is broke up again,*
> *Some second guest to entertain,*
> *(For graves have learn'd that woman-head,*
> *To be to more than one a bed)*
> *And he that digs it, spies*
> *A bracelet of bright hair about the bone,*
> *Will he not let'us alone,*
> *And think that there a loving couple lies,*
> *Who thought that this device might be some way*
> *To make their souls, at the last busy day,*
> *Meet at this grave, and make a little stay?*

Whenever Alba quoted it she skipped the part about graves learning, like women, to be to more than one a bed, and she didn't care for the later stanzas, either. She was moved by the lovers being linked by that bracelet of bright hair, and their hope to find each other on Judgement Day and to stay together, as when they were flesh and blood, before being called up for Judgement. That was in the early years of our marriage when Alba still half-believed in God and didn't believe at all in the Last Judgement.

She had a way of believing, even when she didn't believe, or maybe I should say she was always hopeful — a hopeful skeptic. Take the letter written to little Skye, when she was six or seven months old, by the priest who baptized her. That was Father Brocard, of the Carmelite Fathers, and in his letter he explained to Skye that she had become an heiress, an adopted child of God, with a right to heaven. I had read the letter and had thought it a fond gesture, but then Alba read it aloud to me, choosing certain passages, like when Father Brocard tells Skye, *I put a pinch of salt in your mouth and asked that it preserve for you a taste for divine things, for heavenly wisdom. With exorcisms I bade Satan, in the name of the Holy Trinity, depart and not molest you. And as a sign of the struggle you will have with the power of evil during life, I anointed you with oil, as formerly wrestlers were anointed. Oil makes the body supple and yet difficult for an opponent to hold. Oil is looked upon as conferring strength and giving encouragement.*

"That's beautiful," Alba said. "I love the idea of Skye having become an heiress. There's poetry in the words and another kind of poetry in the ritual. It doesn't matter that we don't believe the ritual works in some sacramental way. The ritual and what he's saying here is our hope for Skye. I *want* her to have a taste for divine things and heavenly wisdom. I *want* her to be strong and to escape the evil things in life. It's our hope."

We had the same hopes and desires, Alba and I.

☙

Leo Conti took me out to lunch at Fête Champêtre and gave me a check for two of my frescos, the pair he had snatched before I could smash them to bits. He had made off with them two or more years ago and I had forgotten about it, so the money was like a gift. The envelope with the check also contained an accounting statement from the Conti Gallery which would satisfy scrupulous agents of the IRS and the Commonwealth of Massachusetts.

Days later, when I thought about it, it seemed to me that Leo had sold them for about half of what I figured he would have asked from a buyer. Or maybe the accounting statement was, as his defense lawyer might say, the innocent result of sloppy bookkeeping due to distraction from overwork. Or fraud. On the other hand, he had taken care of expenses and provided my exhibit with a catalog beautiful enough to make you sweat, boosting the price of every canvas ten percent, so I decided to forget about it. Some painters market their work themselves, so as not to leave forty or fifty percent with the gallery, while others, like myself, would rather paint than spend time being nice to blind blockheads who think your work is overpriced. Leo and I don't have a written agreement, only an understanding and a handshake. He's all right, mostly. He helped raise me from the dead and I'm painting.

Quincy does a good job at the gallery as she's brought in some younger painters and, more important, younger buyers. She was flat broke and couldn't get a job anywhere when Leo hired her. "But I saw beneath the surface," he told me. "She needed a mentor. She had a good eye, but she needed someone like myself who knows the business side of the art world," he said. He went on to tell me that Quincy's father works in "that building downtown that looks like an old-fashioned washboard."

"That's the Federal Reserve Bank of Boston," I said.

"Is it? I always wondered."

"Leo."

"But I didn't know it at the time, Renato! Or if I did, it meant nothing to me. I brought her in because she's a natural. I could tell."

❧

I know Alba's not coming back, not the way I want her back. I know she's gone. I've always known it. But I always hoped she might come back. I can wait.

❧

So this clumsy scrawl goes limping to its end. I confess it's been pieced together from an old memoir, from jottings on the kitchen calendar, scribbled notes and my defective memory. These past few years I've thought a lot and read a lot and I'm sick to a fare-thee-well of philosophers, cosmologists, theologians and atomists, and their books, books, books. I love the things of this world — yes, the perishing things of this perishing world — and most especially I love the flesh and bone and blood that makes us as we are. I would not be the painter I am if I did not.

I remember from when I was a kid hearing uncles Nicolo and Zitti argue over reality and what was real. Nicolo always said you needed mathematics to find your way to basic reality, and what you found were atoms — a nucleus of protons and neutrons surrounded by a cloud of electrons. But Zitti, who loved words and was skeptical of numbers, believed that atoms and their electrons composed merely the distracting surface of reality or, as I recall him saying, the sensuous fog that hovers over true reality so we can grasp it with our senses. And when they'd turn to my father to settle the dispute, he'd say they should carve stone all day, as he did, to learn about reality.

I suppose both uncles were right, each in his way, but I've always liked most of all my father's common sense of things. I was adopted into the Stillamare family and into this world to live and die here. I never felt like an orphan until now, left on this doorstep to noplace. Getting to the bottom of things with the Large Hadron Collider is certainly worthwhile and it satisfies our innate curiosity to pry and penetrate the world, to find out how it works. But that's the wrong direction to go if you want to get to the meaning of anything. You can't arrive at the meaning of a story by analyzing the words and composing a dictionary or, for those who try to go even deeper, by studying the alphabet. My works are more than paint on canvas, despite the bla-bla-bla of certain moronic theorists. You can't understand anything unless you get your arms around it and grab it whole, and sometimes the whole is large, very large.

As uncle Nicolo said, atoms are very strange — you blast them open and all these particles fly out, like a clock with too many parts. He spoke those words long ago, when MIT was doing atomic research with a Van de Graaff generator, a machine that creates lightning bolts the same way pulling a wool blanket from your bed in winter generates sparks. Nowadays, physicists have exquisitely sophisticated, powerful equipment and can hurl opposing streams of protons into head-on collisions that explode into sizzling bits of energy, thus mimicking the creation of things and the beginning of time. Still, the closer we get to the bottom and beginning, the clearer it becomes that what we take as solid in this world is mutable and evanescent. It comes and goes. Human love is the only thing that lasts, as steady as Mount Monadnock and beautiful as daylight.

❦

The question isn't whether Alba's atoms have dispersed — for certain they have — the question is whether anything remains beyond those dresses in the closet and my memory of her.

🐝

The gods have given us love instead of immortality.

🐝

It would help if you were here and we could talk about the children. Not that anything is wrong. But sometimes I wonder if they know what they're doing. I wouldn't say this to anyone else but, frankly, if two of them are all right you can be sure the third is having some kind of trouble. Not big trouble, but the sort you get when you're naive about life. And yes, I know how old they are. And if you were here you could remind me that they are grown adults — unless you had a worry of your own about them.

🐝

Driving homeward in the middle of this large midsummer day, the sun high and the heat heavy. All along the roadside there was flowering eggs-and-butter, Queen Anne's lace, blue stars of wild chicory, and I had such a longing to walk a ways into a field and lie down under the quiet air, to sleep.

The Author

Eugene Mirabelli is the author of eight previous novels, numerous articles, reviews, interviews and short stories. He has received a Rockefeller Foundation Award, was co-founder and co-director of Alternative Literary Programs in the Schools, and is a professor emeritus of the State University of New York at Albany. He grew up near Boston and that city, and indeed all New England, remains his favorite locale.

The Typeface

William Caslon designed this typeface around 1734 in England and his work soon became popular throughout Europe and the American Colonies where it was a favorite of the printer Benjamin Franklin. It passed out of favor for a time, but revived and is now available in digital form with variations and additions to the original font. This book is printed in Adobe Caslon Pro, closely based on Caslon's specimen pages printed between 1734 and 1770.